Texas Jack came into the trail camp to steal himself a fresh horse. But Will Ambers, the trail boss, caught him in the act and they drew on each other simultaneously. Even while Ambers had the sudden feeling that this outlaw stranger was a certain Confederate war hero he had once known, Texas Jack himself hesitated as he was about to shoot. And that lost instant cost the outlaw his life.

But it left Ambers with a terrible puzzle on his mind and he knew he'd get no rest until he had ferreted out the answer. If Texas Jack was the man he'd thought he was, then who was buried in Captain Ross's honored grave?

To find the answer, Ambers was prepared to face the rising hostility of a Texas town that still cherished the memory of their greatest war hero. Despite the growing danger to himself, Ambers persisted in his search to bring to light the town's guiltiest secret. . . .

Turn this book over for second complete novel

TWO GRAVES FOR A GUNMAN

by Barry Cord

AN ACE BOOK

Ace Publishing Corporation
1120 Avenue of the Americas
New York, N.Y. 10036

I

SOMEWHERE HIGH UP among the lonely, windswept peaks the rider passed into Texas. There were no markers to inform him when he crossed the state line, but he knew the wild country like the back of his hand, although he had not been there for many years.

He was a gaunt, powerful man in his late thirties, still ramrod straight, but graying now at the temples. He was a man haunted by memories.

Up north they knew him as Texas Jack, an outlaw with a price on his head, a man fast and deadly with a gun.

It was not what he had wanted out of life, but it was the way things had turned out.

The big, bay stallion he was riding began to falter on the downslope; great flecks of foam clung to his muzzle. Pity showed in the tired man's eyes. He had pushed the animal hard all the way from Cheyenne, pressed by the three riders he knew were on the trail behind him.

"Easy, boy," he muttered. "Just a little more . . ."

But when the bay stumbled he eased up, knowing there was nothing left in the animal and that this was as far as he could go. He dismounted and leaned wearily against the animal's heaving flank, choking back a bitter disappointment.

The stallion turned to look at him with wide, tortured eyes, and he reacted to the mute appeal. He reached up and patted the sweat-matted muzzle. "All right, boy," he said softly, "no more."

He walked the spent animal toward a clump of jack pine overlooking a narrow valley winding through the hills. A jackdaw scolded him as he came close and then flew off. He paused in the shade and looked beyond the hills and thought of the small town less than thirty miles away.

"Cottonwood Wells." His lips shaped the words, and then he felt a pain in his chest again, and a small fear fluttered through him. He closed his eyes. *Not now,* he thought wildly, *not yet. . . .*

Behind him the bay stood with legs widespread, head drooping. A small breeze ruffled his mane. The animal shivered.

Bracing his back against one of the small trees, Texas Jack squatted on his heels and reached inside his shirt pocket for the makings.

Nothing left to do, he thought, *except to wait here for Lou, Corbin and Parrish.* Once they had been his friends; now they wanted to kill him.

He looked back toward the high ridges from whence he had come.

"I don't have it, Lou," he muttered. "But you won't believe me, will you?"

He stuck the end of his badly-shaped cigarette into a corner of his mouth, his eyes hard, brittle. He could stop Lou and maybe even Corbin, but he couldn't stop all three of them.

He turned his head suddenly, listening as a sound carried to him on the small wind.

Cattle lowing!

It came from somewhere below, lost among the sage-stippled hills flanking the narrow valley.

He surged up to his feet, hope burning through the weariness in his face. Cattle meant drovers, *horses!*

He put a hand on the bay's drooping neck. "Come on, boy," he said harshly, "looks like we're gonna find you a home."

They started down the slope, heading for the sound of cattle moving through the hills toward them.

II

WILL AMBERS sat in the saddle of his Roman-nosed roan and watched the longhorns as they jostled one another, moving through the narrow pass.

They were ten days out and the cattle drive was already in trouble, he thought morosely, and tried to shake off the feeling of uneasiness that had crept up on him through the day. He was responsible for two thousand head of mixed steers, representing the hopes and financial fortunes of a half-dozen Texas cattlemen; he had two thousand head of beef with more than a thousand miles of wild and unsettled country to traverse.

Will shifted in his saddle and looked down the high pass, waiting for Rollins to show up with the remuda. Will was a tall, saddle-hardened man with a lean, intelligent face and a shock of brown, unruly hair. He was twenty-five, a little young to be trail boss of a herd this size. However, those who worked with him didn't think so, nor had the men who had entrusted their cattle and their hopes to him. They knew Will Ambers as a thoughtful, capable man who, once set upon a venture, would see it through, come hell, high water or blizzard.

It was quite possible he'd have to fight his way through all three before he reached the mining camps on the Pacific side of the Rockies with this herd.

A shout pulled his attention away from the steers. He turned and rode to the rider waiting for him on a knoll overlooking the wider valley beyond.

Buck Stevens was fifty-six, a craggy-faced, tough, white-thatched man who twice had been wiped out by Texas weather, once by drought and once by blizzard. The five hundred head he had in this drive represented his last chance at survival.

Will said, "How's the cavvy holding out?"

Buck turned to look toward the small band of horses being driven toward them.

"Footsore, but holding up." He looked Will in the eye.

"That's what I want to talk to you about. We've got to rest them, or half of them will go lame on us before the week is out."

Will shook his head. "We haven't got the time." He nodded toward the western rises, his tone hardening. "We've got to make Big Springs before the middle of June. The water holes start drying up then."

Buck worked his chew of tobacco thoughtfully into a corner of his cheek and spat over his horse's ear. "I know horses," he said bluntly, "horses an' cows. That's about all I know." He indicated the cavvy coming up behind the last steers. "Yo're gonna have to rest them horses, or we'll be walking this herd across the mountains."

"We'll rest them at Big Springs," Will said. He looked up at the sky. "Be dark in an hour. Let's get the herd bedded down in the valley ahead."

The first stars gleamed brightly in the sky as the mixed steers began to settle down. It looked like a quiet night.

The drovers crowded around the chuck wagon, received their shares of stew and biscuits and drifted off around the fire to eat. A coyote cried somewhere in the dark hills and was joined by another. Both suddenly broke off.

Will heard the labored breathing of a horse in the darkness. He glanced at Buck, who nodded and said quietly, "Looks like we got company coming."

The men kept eating, but there was an alertness in

their manner now and they kept looking in the direction of the oncoming horse.

It was a dark bulk at first, a shapeless blob moving toward them. Then man and horse came within the range of the camp fire and paused. No one said anything for a moment. Finally Will waved a hand toward the coffee pot on a rock by the fire.

"Coffee, stranger?"

Texas Jack nodded. "Much obliged." His voice was easy but his stride was tired as he let his horse stand where it had stopped and came toward the fire. He hunkered down between Will and Buck; Buck handed him a tin cup and watched as the gaunt man poured his coffee.

"Come far?"

Texas Jack nodded. "Heard your drive while I was up in the hills, heading east." He turned to Will, who was eyeing him. His tone hardened slightly. "Something about me bothering you, fella?"

Will's answer was considered. "You look like a man I once knew, a Captain Ross, Seventh Texas Volunteers."

Texas Jack studied Will for a moment and then shook his head. "Sorry to disappoint you. Never was in the Army." He turned back to Buck. "I'm on my way to Cotton Wells, small town less than thirty miles from here. You must have passed it."

Buck said: "Could have. We didn't see it."

Jack took a sip of his coffee. "I'm in a bit of a hurry. Like to trade horses—anything that will get me there will do."

Will said evenly, "Sorry. We need every horse we've got."

Texas Jack swung around to him, frowning. Then he looked at Buck.

Buck said: "I'm Buck Stevens. He's Will Ambers, trail boss."

Texas Jack knuckled the stubble on his jaw. "Would have figured it the other way around." To Will he said, "Sorry." But his smile was cold and there was no sorry in it. "I still need a mount. I'll leave you mine. He's easy worth two of anything you've brought along."

Will eyed the spent animal on the outer edge of the firelight. He said slowly, "A month out in pasture, maybe, if he isn't wind-broke."

Texas Jack slowly set his cup down and straightened, the silver handle of his Colt catching the flame glow. He looked dangerous as he eyed Will and the other men around the camp fire.

"I need a horse real bad," he said quietly. "I'll pay you."

Will got to his feet. Buck's hand drifted down to his gun butt. One of the drovers near the chuck wagon reached for his rifle.

Will's voice was even. "Mister, I'd loan you a horse, if I could spare him. I can't!"

Texas Jack studied the quiet men around the camp fire for a long moment and then shrugged. He hunkered down again and picked up his cup. The men around the fire relaxed slightly.

"Guess you mean it," he said. He looked toward the

dark hills, but his face showed only a deep weariness. "Mind if I spend the night here? Maybe the rest will do my horse good."

"Suit yourself," Will replied. He added, "We've got grub to spare. You're welcome to stew and biscuits."

He watched Texas Jack get up and lead his stallion toward the picket line. He gave the animal some water, but the horse was too tired to eat. Will knew that the stallion would be no good, ever.

He wondered what had driven this man so hard.

Buck's voice intruded, "I'll be glad when he's gone, Will."

Will frowned. "Know him?"

Buck nodded. "Texas Jack. Saw posters up in Montana, Nevada, California: one thousand dollars reward." He shrugged. "A lot of money for a man, but not many who care to give it a try."

Will knuckled his jaw. "You might be wrong." He looked toward Texas Jack, who was walking toward the chuck wagon. "I'd swear he was Captain Ross. One of the most decorated men on the southern front, just over five years ago."

Buck shrugged. "Could be both." His voice lowered. "Don't push him, Will. You're nowhere near as good with a handgun."

Will got to his feet and stretched. "Get some sleep. I'll take the first watch."

The cattle settled quietly. It was a still, crisp night, and sounds carried a long way in the darkness. The wind came down from the mountains and ran careless fingers over the men sleeping curled up in their blankets around the dying fire. The soft chanting of the riders on night watch drifted over them.

Texas Jack lay with his head on his saddle and stared up at the stars. He was bone tired, but he wasn't sleepy, and he had never intended to sleep. He stirred slightly and looked across the dark ground to the motionless bodies of the men beyond the chuck wagon. Some of them snored softly, others more loudly and raspingly. All of them were exhausted and none of them stirred.

Texas Jack eyed the darkness that hid the high pass and thought bitterly of the thirty miles between him and Cottonwood Wells.

A sound drifted down from the higher ridges, tensing him. He waited a long moment, but it was not repeated. He did not relax. Lou, Corbin and Parrish would be coming tomorrow, if not tonight. He knew he couldn't wait.

He lifted himself slowly to one elbow. No one stirred among the sleeping men.

He raised himself slowly to his feet, buckled on his gun belt and picked up his boots. He did not put them on. Holding them in his left hand, he moved quietly toward the horses picketed under the trees.

Andy White, the night guard, sat with his back against the bole of a live oak, the twist of a cigarette limp between his teeth. There was no danger from Indians and the cavvy was tired, only a prowling lobo or cougar might cause alarm and panic among the tired horses.

Andy dozed. He was sixteen years old and this was his first trip with a trail drive and the excitement had taken its toll.

He didn't see the gaunt man who paused in the shadows to eye the horses tied to the picket line. He stirred slightly and the cigarette clung to his lower lip as his mouth opened and he sighed deeply.

Texas Jack swung toward him. He slipped his gun from his holster and held it ready. The boy stirred again. Then his breathing deepened and Texas Jack slowly lowered his gun.

He walked swiftly to the picket line and picked out a big roan stallion. The animal snorted softly as he came close; his hand shot out, his fingers clamping over the animal's muzzle and stifling further sound.

"Easy, feller," he breathed. "I ain't gonna hurt you."

The horse trembled. Texas Jack eased his grip and slipped into his worn boots. He wouldn't need his saddle. He couldn't take the time, or the risk, to fetch it. It was only thirty miles to Cottonwood Wells; he could ride the roan bareback that far.

He untied the big animal and started to lead him from among the others.

Will's voice from the darkness behind him was cold. "I wouldn't, Captain."

Texas Jack stopped, his back to Will. He stood this way for a long, silent moment, debating his course of action; then he turned.

Will Ambers stood a few feet away with a gun in his

14

hand. Will said, "Take your horse and go, Captain. Leave the roan!"

Texas Jack shook his head. "I've got to get to Cottonwood Wells. Don't try to stop me."

Roused by the sound of voices, Andy stirred. He saw Texas Jack by the picket line and started to reach for his rifle.

Texas Jack's voice whipped at him, flat and hard. "Leave that gun alone, boy!"

Andy's hand jerked back from the rifle; he stared wide-eyed at Will.

Will said carefully, "Captain, I wish I could help you. But I can't let you take that horse. We're short now; we lose one more and we're in trouble."

"You're in trouble now," the gaunt man said. His voice had flattened. "Make a move to stop me and I'll kill you both."

He started to lead the roan away from the trees. Will bit his lips and cocked his gun.

"Dammit, Captain—I can't—"

Texas Jack whirled and went for his holstered gun. He had his hand on the butt before Will pulled the trigger. Then, for a strange and inexplicable moment, he paused. Will fired.

The bullet drove Texas Jack around and down. He stirred once as Will walked to him. He tried to roll over; then he sighed and went still.

Will looked down at the dead man; there was a sick feeling in the pit of his stomach. He had fired almost without thought and there was no anger in him, nor satisfaction. There was only an odd confusion, as though somehow he had been forced to kill a friend.

Andy stared from the shadows; his eyes were round and there was an uneasy feeling at the pit of his stomach. This was the first man he had seen killed.

The shot had roused the sleeping drovers. They came running toward the picket line, Buck leading with a rifle in his hands.

Buck stopped as he saw Will and Andy, then came slowly, as the others crowded behind him to look down at the body of Texas Jack.

"Tried to steal a horse," Will said, tonelessly. "I killed him."

Buck looked at Will. "I never saw him in action," he said slowly. "But he had a bad reputation with a gun."

"He didn't have a chance," Will cut in harshly. "I had a gun on him." He shook his head. "Maybe I should have let him take the roan, Buck."

"Glad you didn't."

Buck turned to the men behind them. "Someone put a blanket over the body." He turned to Andy. "You, boy—you stand watch over him. We'll bury him at sunup."

III

THE DEAD MAN'S gun lay on the blanket alongside his scuffed cartridge belt, sixty cents in change and a tattered wallet holding only the faded picture of a woman and two small children. It was not a good picture and it must have been taken a long time ago. The man who had died must have treasured it.

"Not much to show for a man's life," Will said slowly. He was standing with Buck, looking down at the blanket spread out beside the grave. "A gun and sixty cents . . ." He lifted his gaze to Texas Jack's horse, standing just beyond. His head was drooping; he was wind-broken. Somehow he was a mute testimony to the meaninglessness of the man's death.

Something nagged at Will and made him lift his gaze toward the distant peaks. "I wonder who he really was, Buck."

Buck shrugged. "Reckon we'll never know."

He started to turn away. The herd was already on the move, heading up the narrow valley. They had a long, long way to go.

But Will remained beside the side of the grave, eyeing the cross he had hammered into the earth at the

17

head of it. Texas Jack was whittled into it, with the date the man had died, June 2, 1870.

The southwest is dotted with the graves of unknown men, he thought. *Why is this one different?*

Buck had paused by his horse. "He's dead, Will." He was impatient to get going. "There's nothing more we can do for him now."

"Someone's probably waiting for him in Cottonwood Wells," Will said slowly. "That woman, maybe those kids." He shook his head and looked toward the hills through which they had come. He knew he could not let the man lie in a shallow grave, to be forgotten.

"The sheriff should be notified, too."

Buck put a hand on the trail boss's shoulder. "I know how you feel, Will. But some things happen, they just sort of happen." He looked down at the grave. "You killed a horse thief, a man with a price on his head up north. You don't owe him anything, and we don't have the time to make anything more of it."

"I'll have to make the time," Will said. "I have to know who he is, Buck."

Buck studied the younger man for a moment, sensing the stubbornness in Will, the feeling of guilt. He sighed deeply and nodded.

"We should make the river in three days. I'll rest the cattle and the horses a day. Join us there."

Will picked up Texas Jack's wallet and studied the picture of the woman and the two small children for a long moment, then tucked it away in his pocket. Texas Jack's mount was saddled and waiting. He lifted his head as Will approached with the dead man's cartridge belt and holster. The oiled and shiny silver-handled gun glinted in the early-morning light. Will hung the gun belt from the bay's saddle horn.

The horse would never be any good again, but he couldn't leave the animal to die, and Buck couldn't take him with them. If he took it easy, Will thought, the bay could make it to Cottonwood Wells with him.

He mounted his roan and swung around to pick up the bay's trailing reins.

Buck said gruffly, "Good luck, Will."

Will waved. "I'll meet you at the river." He turned away, the bay trailing behind.

Buck watched until Will had passed out of sight through the canyon pass. Behind him the cattle were already on the move.

He mounted and rode to join them, but he looked back once uneasily to the grave on the side of the hill.

It was mid-afternoon when Will came upon a small road sign that read, "Cottonwood Wells, 5 miles." It was an old sign, weathered and barely decipherable, and the road that led toward low, rolling hills showed little signs of recent traffic.

Maybe from the east, Will thought, *but not from this direction....*

Feeling the sun hot on his back, he took a drink from his canteen. The bay stood with head down, glad of the rest. The butt of the gun in Texas Jack's holster held Will's attention. The gun was the only thing of value the dead man had left behind; obviously prized, it had been well kept. There were crossed sabers etched into the silver butt plates.

He had seen the gun before. It had been worn by a ramrod-straight man he had met briefly during the War, a man named Captain Ross.

He swung around the sign and headed for the town behind the rolling hills.

Will heard the school bell before he came upon it. It was clanging for order, an end to recess. He could hear the faint whooping of children playing. Then, coming around a bend, he pulled up as two freckle-faced children, one a girl about nine and the other a boy about seven, darted across the road.

They stopped on the other side and eyed him solemnly. The boy leveled a wooden pistol and said, "Bang, Bang." He looked disappointed as Will remained in the saddle, smiling at him.

The boy moved into the road, wary but emboldened by Will's friendly appearance. The girl remained behind, a bit fearful. She said, "Timmy, you come here."

Timmy moved close to the bay trailing Will. He pointed to the gun hanging from the saddle. "Can I try it, mister?"

Will shook his head. "I'm afraid it's a little too big for you to handle, sonny."

He turned as a man came out of the school yard and called sharply, "Timmy, Susie! Didn't you hear the bell?"

Timmy backed slowly to join his sister; then the two of them scampered past the man into the school yard.

The schoolmaster looked at Will. He had a thatch of prematurely white hair and bright, blue eyes. His left sleeve dangled at his side, empty.

"Guns and war," he said bitterly. "It's only been five years since Appomatox and already the children—"

He broke off, his attention caught by the gun hanging from the bay's saddle. His glance to Will now was sharp and questioning.

"I'm Ralph Teacher. Can I be of any help?"

"I'm looking for the sheriff."

Teacher's gaze moved back to the riderless, foot-sore horse behind Will. He took a long moment before answering, and Will had the feeling the man was weighing his words.

"Sheriff's office is in Rawlings, forty miles south of here, mister—"

"Ambers," Will said. "I'm with a trail herd passing by." He frowned. "Can't take the time to go to Rawlings. Is there any law in Cottonwood Wells?"

Teacher said, "Jack Thomas, town marshal, tax collector—an ambitious man with nowhere to go."

"Hard man to get along with?"

Teacher shrugged. "Not if you agree with him." He flicked a glance to the riderless horse again. "Trouble on the drive, Mr. Ambers?"

Will sidestepped the question. "Where can I find the marshal?"

Teacher gestured toward a group of dusty trees shadowing the bend in the road ahead.

"Small office, just across the town square, directly south of the Ross Memorial."

Will stiffened slightly and frowned.

"Ross Memorial?"

Teacher glanced at him, a curious light in his eyes. A small racket from inside the schoolhouse distracted him.

"I'll have to go," he said. He gestured again. "You can't miss it, once you get to the square." He turned away. "If Thomas ain't there, try Tony's Pool Hall."

Will watched him for a moment before riding on.

IV

THE THREE RIDERS paused high in the hills, a few miles inside the Texas line. They were trailing three spare horses and one of the animals carried supplies.

Two of them remained mounted; the other got down and knelt by the hoof prints of a horse in a patch of sandy soil.

All three men were armed with rifles and handguns; they had the hard, restless look of men who used guns for a living.

Lou Stillman, Parrish and Corbin—a man could retire on the collective reward offered for them.

Corbin straightened from examining the hoof prints.

He walked slowly toward a sapling and touched the dried flecks of foam still clinging to the twigs. His gaze picked up boot prints beside the hoof prints just beyond. He turned and walked quickly back to his companions. Half Indian, he was wire hard and tough, with straight coal-black hair under which light blue eyes made a disconcerting contrast.

He said, "We've run him into the ground, Lou. He can't be more than a few miles down the slope, and he's afoot."

Corbin's speech was slow and guttural. It had town Indian in it: greasy blanket and prideless. Corbin was neither; he could do better when he wanted to. But he didn't care.

Lou took a long swallow from his canteen.

"That big bay held up longer than I thought," he said. Lou was a stocky man, light brown hair falling long and curly down his neck; a thick, brown mustache dominated his face. It was hard to tell how old he was. He was a hard man, slow to speak and of unshakable opinions.

"Never figured Texas Jack the kind to run out on us," Parrish said. He was a tall, thin man who looked like a schoolteacher when he put on his steel-rimmed spectacles; he wore a shoulder holster under his coat. He shook his head, looking doleful. "Never figured him that kind at all."

"A woman," Lou speculated. Something dark and bitter stirred in his voice as he said this, and Parrish looked at him sharply, wondering at the odd hate in the man.

23

"Must have been a woman; why else would he have crossed us?"

Parrish shrugged. He dismounted, stretched his leg muscles and reached for his canteen. He moved off a bit, staring down slope.

"What woman, Lou?"

Lou shook his head. "He never said, but he had a picture with him: woman and a couple of kids. And he came from Texas, someplace around here—"

The warning sound of a rattler and Corbin's move to his knife were simultaneous. The blade glinted in the sunlight, and the nearly decapitated snake writhed in the rocks a few feet from Parrish.

Parrish looked at it; then in reaction he drew and fired his shoulder gun, emptying it into the rattler, tearing it to chunks of flesh.

Lou said coldly, "Waste of shells."

Parrish took a deep breath. "Hell with the shells!" He reloaded and looked across to Corbin, who had retrieved his knife and was casually wiping it on his pant leg.

"Thanks," he said.

Corbin's blue eyes appraised him mildly. "*De nada.*" He shrugged.

Corbin had been born and brought up along the New Mexican-Mexican border. He didn't know his parents and never tried to find out who they were. He had been raised in an army post by an old Apache scout, but he had been accepted by neither the military nor

24

the Apaches, and when he was fourteen he had drifted away.

He had no goals; he lived day by day.

"It's not the money so much," Lou said. "I trusted him." He looked at Parrish and at Corbin. "I'd like to know why."

They rode down the hill together with the sun low behind them.

The trail herd was bedded down by a small stream when the two riders came upon it. They moved in at sundown, outlined against the darkening sky; they did not try to hide their coming.

Talking to the remuda boss, Hanson, Buck swung around and waited for them. The men near the chuck wagon edged closer to their rifles.

Lou and Parrish rode up to the camp fire; they remained in their saddles, their hands crossed on the saddle horns. Lou glanced casually over the men by the chuck wagon.

"Howdy," Lou said pleasantly.

Buck studied him for a moment, then shifted his gaze to Parrish. He had seen both these men somewhere, he thought—or seen pictures of them. Like Texas Jack, they were quiet, deadly men.

Up on the slope behind Parrish he thought he saw movement. Something glinted very briefly, and he knew it was a hidden rifle.

Buck's face didn't show what he knew.

"Just bedding down for the night," he said. He motioned to the coffee pot. "Coffee?"

Parrish started to shake his head, but Lou said pleasantly, "Much obliged to you." He swung down and tied his horse to the wagon wheel, and after a brief moment Parrish joined him.

They squatted by the fire. Lou made a motion toward the cattle. "Taking them to Dodge?"

"Nevada gold fields," Buck answered.

Lou showed his surprise. "Just came from there," he said. "Them miners can use the beef, that's for sure." He sucked at his coffee, his eyes thoughtful. "We're looking for a friend of ours. Tall man riding a bay horse?"

Buck didn't answer right away.

Parrish said, "His horse was in bad shape. We thought he might have tried to make a trade for one of yours."

Buck shook his head. "Didn't see him."

Lou studied him for a moment, then shifted his attention to the men around the wagon. He shrugged. "Guess he went the other way." He finished his coffee and stood up. "Just in case you see him, though, tell him Lou and Parrish are looking for him."

Buck nodded.

Lou and Parrish climbed into their saddles. Lou waved. "Thanks for the coffee."

Buck remained hunkered by the fire as they rode off. Hanson and one of the drovers walked to him. Hanson looked after the departing men and said, "There was a man on the slope, Buck. He was looking over the remuda."

"Had a gun on us, too," Buck said. He stood up, stretching cramped leg muscles. He was worried about Will. If these men were friends of Texas Jack, then Will was in trouble.

A quarter of a mile from the trail camp Parrish and Lou pulled up and waited for Corbin. The half-breed joined them a few minutes later.

Parrish asked: "No sign of the bay?"

Corbin shook his head.

"They didn't have the money, either," Lou said. His voice was thoughtful. "I could smell it. Thirty thousand dollars is hard to hide."

Parrish's voice was bitter. "Then who?"

Corbin said, "Let's get back to the grave."

It was close to midnight when they pulled up by Texas Jack's grave. A half moon in a cloudless sky cast enough light for Corbin to study tracks just beyond the freshly turned earth. They had come upon the grave in the morning and dug into it enough to make sure it was Texas Jack who was buried there.

Corbin came back to where Parrish and Lou were looking down on the grave.

"Like I said this morning—a rider, leading Jack's bay, headed east."

Lou nodded. "Had to make sure . . . could have been a blind lead to throw us off."

Parrish was looking down at the tilted sign. "Texas Jack was good with a gun. Wonder how he got it?"

"Everybody makes a mistake some time," Lou muttered. "Texas Jack made two: once crossing us, the other running into the man who killed him."

V

THE ROSS MEMORIAL was set in the middle of the town square, on a patch of green grass cut short and enclosed by links of heavy anchor chain, which were painted black and strung from iron post to iron post. A small wreath of bright-colored straw flowers lay against the base of the memorial.

It was a monolith of granite roughly shaped on three sides and glass smooth on the other. Into the stone, just above the chiseled inscription and as if thrust into it by an angry and powerful man, was a cavalry saber; only the handle and four inches of the blade showed.

Under it was the neatly chiseled lettering:

IN PROUD AND GRATEFUL
RECOGNITION OF
WESLEY P. ROSS, CAPT. CSA

Will Ambers studied the inscription, trying to make it fit the man he had killed. No one bothered him. The town square drowsed in the afternoon sun; old trees lined the square. Cottonwood Wells was an old town as Texas towns went; it had a settled, peaceful look that even the recent war had not disturbed.

Behind Will the wind-broken stallion stood, his head drooping. The gun hanging from his saddle seemed a mute testimony to what Will was seeking here.

In the bank across the street, Nathan Forge came out of his private office. It was still close to an hour before closing time, but there was no one inside the bank except a woman at the window, looking out into the square. Something about her stance brought an alarmed frown to his eyes; he strode quickly to her and looked out, seeing Will just as he started to ride past the memorial toward the law office on the far side of the square.

Nathan watched for a moment, his lean face sober and thoughtful. He was a good-looking man in his middle thirties; he was single and quietly forceful, but not very ambitious.

The woman uttered a small sigh and turned toward Nathan; there was fear in her eyes.

"Nathan?"

He turned to her. They eyed each other for a long moment, sharing a mute dread. "I'll see what he wants," Nathan said.

He walked quickly to the door and went out. The woman remained by the window, her face beginning to crumple.

Will Ambers tied up in front of the sign that read: "Town Marshal" and went inside, finding the door unlocked. The office was a cubbyhole, untidy and empty.

He stood a moment undecided, knowing that he could not spend too much time in Cottonwood Wells and that he had to be getting back to the trail herd.

He started to turn away, but stopped as he heard a step behind him.

Nathan Forge paused in the doorway. "Can I be of help, mister?"

"Will Ambers," Will said shortly. "I'm looking for the marshal."

"He just stepped out." Nathan smiled. "Something I can do for you?"

"I'm in a hurry," Will said. "I'm with a trail herd north of here."

"I envy you, then," Nathan said. "Your freedom, your travels—my job's far more prosaic, I'm afraid. I'm the town banker; Nathan Forge."

"There are times when I'd trade with you," Will said. He walked to the door and looked outside. "Know where I can find the marshal?"

Nathan shrugged. "Jack could be anywhere in town. Mostly, though, he kills time playing pool in Tony's place on Sundown Street." He paused. "Is your business urgent, Mr. Ambers?"

"I think it is," Will replied. He moved past the banker and stopped by the hitchrack to untie his horse.

Nathan watched him from the office doorway. "I saw you stop by the memorial out there," he said quietly. "Did you know Captain Ross?"

"Only by reputation."

Nathan nodded. "Most people do. Captain Ross was

one of the finest men I knew; I rode with him under Jubal Early."

Nathan paused and looked across the square to the memorial. "He was also one of the South's most decorated men, Mr. Ambers, and this town will always remember him with great pride. He was born here, you know—raised on a small farm just a few miles away."

He turned and eyed Will. "When did you meet him?"

"Once, at the battle of Bent's Ford." Will looked across his saddle to the block of stone on the patch of green grass; he was trying to square this with what he now knew of the man; there was a long gap between.

"I ran into Captain Ross again yesterday, just off the old Comanche trail. He was headed this way."

Nathan stiffened; then slowly he started to shake his head. "No," he said. "I'm afraid you—"

"He was trying to steal one of our horses." Will cut him off coldly. "I had to kill him!"

Wordless and shocked Nathan stared at him.

Will mounted. "I'll go find the marshal." He swung his horse away from the hitchrack, the bay trailing.

Nathan watched him ride away. "Thank God," he said. It was a heartfelt, bitter whisper. "Thank God!"

But he wondered how he was going to tell the woman waiting for him in the bank.

Tony's Pool Hall was on an off street, flanked by a derelict structure on one side and a saddle shop on the other. It was never very busy, but there was always someone there, whiling away the time at the tables.

The long, narrow room had a small bar which served only beer, and two pool tables, only one of which was in use when Will Ambers paused just inside the doorway. A few loungers were watching Jack Thomas, a big, beefy man in his late twenties, rack up a score against his opponent. The badge on his vest glittered brightly from constant polishing; obviously it meant a lot to him. In other respects, Thomas was a careless, sloppy dresser.

For all his bulk, the town marshal was a man of surprising grace and agility, and he was playing a great game of eight ball.

He leaned over the table, angled his position and said confidently, "Two bank shot, corner pocket." He made his shot and reached up with his cue to click his tally on the overhead wire.

Will studied him for a moment, then walked to the pool table. Thomas had his back to him; he was squinting down the table, surveying his next shot.

Will tapped him on the shoulder. "Marshal Thomas?"

Thomas reached back and made an impatient, silencing wigwag behind him.

Will shrugged and waited.

Thomas made his shot and turned to face him with a truculent scowl.

"All right, mister, what's rushing you?"

Will held down his rising temper. "Nothing that can't wait until you're through here."

He started to leave. Thomas grabbed him by the arm and pulled him around.

"Now hold on, fella. You don't look like a miner, nor

a farmer, either." He glanced at Will's gun. "Heard there was a trail herd going through on the old Comanche trail. You with them?"

Will nodded.

"Well, what do you want to see me about?"

Will's voice was short. There was a lackadaisical attitude in the town, in this man, that irritated him.

"It's customary to report a killing to the law, I understand."

Thomas eyed him closely. "Who was killed? Someone on your train?"

Will shook his head. He glanced at the other men in the room, remembering the memorial in the small dusty square of Cottonwood Wells.

"Wesley Ross!"

Thomas stared blankly at him. No one moved, reacted.

"He tried to steal one of our horses," Will said grimly. "I had to kill him."

Thomas looked him over slowly, puzzled; he was trying to make him out. The others edged closer, hemming Will in.

"He's buried in a shallow grave just off the trail," Will said. "He was headed this way when it happened." He added coldly, "I just thought you ought to know."

Thomas sneered now, his eyes hostile. He lifted his cue and pointed to the door with it. He said with harsh, controlled anger, *"Get out of here!"*

Will didn't move. "I didn't know he was from Cottonwood Wells until I saw the memorial in the square."

Thomas cut him off. "You didn't know, eh? You killed somebody out there, somebody who tried to steal a horse. Then you ride in here with a story about it being Wesley Ross!" His voice choked with bitter anger. "Now come on, mister, just what are you after? Money or glory?"

Will looked at him, puzzled. He could sense the hostility in the others, their sneering judgment.

"I'm not after anything," he said. "The reward money's yours, if you want it. The glory, too, if you want to claim it!"

Stan Walker, the man Thomas had been playing, pushed up beside the marshal. Stan was a rangy, hard-boned farmer in his middle thirties, red-haired and hot-tempered.

"What's he talking about, Jack?"

"Nothing that makes sense," the marshal answered. He turned to Will, his voice roughening. "What reward money?"

"For Wesley Ross," Will said coldly. "Known as Texas Jack up north. He was worth at least five thousand dollars, dead or alive, in a half-dozen counties in California, Nevada and Montana."

The men around Will stared at him, their hostility naked. One of them said angrily, "Jack, let's just throw him out."

Thomas waved him to silence. He looked hard at Will, and sneered. "You telling us that Captain Ross was an outlaw, a killer?"

"One of the worst, and maybe the most dangerous—"

Stan was still holding onto his cue. He shoved the

marshal aside and took a swing at Will's head with it. Will ducked and backed away; his hand dropped warningly to his gun butt.

"Easy, feller."

Stan's voice rang with a wild anger. "Nobody's gonna talk like that to me about the Captain, Jack!"

The marshal gave a flat order. "Hold it, Stan." As the others pressed toward Will, he muttered angrily, "All of you!"

He waited until they had quieted down; then he pointed to the door. "Come on," he said to Will. "I want to show you something."

Will shook his head. "I saw the memorial. I heard about his war record." He paused, knowing he had not been wrong about Captain Ross and Texas Jack; but he did not know why.

He added slowly, "It doesn't change what Ross became later."

Thomas eyed Will with thin contempt.

"You still don't know, do you?"

Will frowned.

"Come on," Thomas said harshly. "It's only a five minute walk from here."

Puzzled, Will nodded. He followed the marshal outside, the others surging out and falling behind them.

VI

NATHAN FORGE stood in his office doorway and watched the woman behind the teller's cage count money and replace currency and change in her till. She made notations on a small pad, but he could see that her mind was not on what she was doing.

She looks suddenly older today, he thought. Knowing what was troubling her, he felt a small and bitter anger.

She was still a fine figure of a woman, still the most beautiful girl in the county. He thought so unreservedly, he had always thought so and the fact that she had been married to someone else had not changed his feelings. In her late twenties the freshness had gone from her face; caring for two children had matured her and deepened a quiet dignity Nathan had always found attractive.

Watching her, the banker felt an aching regret that there was little he could do for her. When she paused and brushed the back of her hand across her eyes he stepped out of his office and went to her.

She looked up as she heard him approach and then looked quickly away, not wanting him to see her as she was. There was no one else in the bank. Midweek was usually very quiet; most of the bank's business was conducted on Fridays and Saturdays when the farmers, small ranchers and miners from as far away as forty miles came to town.

Nathan smiled at her. "Go on home, Marilyn. I'll take care of things at the window until closing time."

Marilyn shook her head. She kept her face averted from him, looking toward the street window.

"What does that man know about my husband, Nathan?"

"Mr. Ambers?" Nathan shrugged. "Nothing."

"He stopped at the memorial."

"Most people do," Nathan said. Gently he pulled her around to face him. "I know how you feel, but I don't think Mr. Ambers will make any trouble."

He paused and looked past her to the street; something was nagging at him.

"It's not Ambers I'm worried about, Marilyn."

She looked up quickly, searching his face. "Who, then?"

Nathan didn't answer for a moment. "Maybe I'm worried over nothing, maybe we both are."

He closed the till and motioned toward the door. "Go on, the children will be coming home soon. Get some rest before they do."

Marilyn shook her head, her eyes holding his. "He was looking for Thomas. Is that who you're worried over, the marshal?"

Nathan shrugged. "Jack's a bad loser, Marilyn; and you

know how he felt about your husband. If he should find out the truth—"

Marilyn nodded; her voice was tired, dispirited. "I know. But Jack doesn't know." She was silent for a moment, her eyes bitter. "All these years, Nathan, these long, trying years. Maybe it would have been better if you—if both of us had—"

Nathan interrupted her, his voice hard, "Had run away?" He shook his head. "Look, Marilyn, that trail boss killed a horse thief on the old Comanche Trail, a man he *thought* was Captain Ross!" He looked to the window again. "He'll tell Jack about it and then he'll ride back to rejoin his trail herd and that will be the end of it."

"What if he doesn't leave?"

"He'll go!" He looked at her now, his voice softening. "Why should he want to stay? He's got problems of his own."

Marilyn lowered her head and sighed deeply. "I don't know. It's just a feeling I have, watching him—the way he looked at the memorial."

Nathan smiled reassuringly. "Shush, Marilyn. No more of that." He saw the tears start in her eyes and he said gently, "I know, I know; it's haunted us both for five years. But we knew, some day, something like this would happen. Now, let me handle it."

Marilyn began to tremble. "Nathan—"

He cut her off. "Get some rest. I'll take care of things with the marshal, and with Mr. Ambers."

Marilyn hesitated, then nodded. "All right, Nathan."

She took her hat from the rack and left the bank. Nathan watched her cross the square from the window; some of the assurance he had shown the woman fading from his face.

The small cemetery looked down on the town from a knoll south of it. Most of the markers were small wood headboards, some of them faded beyond reading. Many of the buried were children, for life was hard on the frontier and medicine was still anchored to medieval methods.

Dominating the cemetery was an imposing granite stone surrounded by a small iron fence. A faded Confederate flag fluttered bravely in the breeze.

The epitaph was simple:

CAPTAIN WESLEY P. ROSS
1838 — 1866
Rest in Peace

Flanked by Marshal Thomas and several of the pool players, Will Ambers stood before the grave.

"He was killed five years ago, trying to save the payroll of the Blackjack Silver Mine," Thomas said. He turned to face Ambers, his face hard. "The Captain's widow lives in a house on Alamo Road. After seeing this, you still figger to tell her her husband was a horse thief, that you just killed him out there on the old Comanche Trail?"

Not speaking, Ambers studied the headstone. A grave is a difficult barrier to overcome.

He took in a long breath. "Yes, I think I will."

He turned and started to walk back to town. Thomas watched him for a moment, his face ugly. His hand went down to rest on his gun.

"Mr. Ambers!"

Will paused. He turned slowly to look back at that small group of hostile men.

"Leave Mrs. Ross alone!" Thomas said.

Ambers studied him for a moment, then turned and kept walking toward town.

VII

THE ROSS HOUSE was on a quiet side street. It was a neat, small, clapboard building, recently painted and enclosed by a four-foot picket fence. A lop-eared, sad-eyed dog (a hound of some sort) lay dozing, tied by a length of rope to a doghouse.

He roused now as Will rode up with the wind-broken bay still trailing. The hound began to bark, his tail wagging happily; he was lonely when the Ross kids were away.

Will dismounted by the closed gate and stood for a

moment looking at the house, not liking what he had to do. He took a deep breath, opened the gate and went up to the front door.

Inside the house Marilyn lay fully clothed on her bed. Her eyes were closed and a wet handkerchief, folded into a long pad, lay across her aching eyes. She had been crying, and she was not asleep. She heard the dog bark before Will came to the door and her body went rigid with dread. She lay there for a long moment as Ambers knocked and knocked again.

She didn't want to answer the door. She didn't want to face anyone, but she knew she would have to. She sat up, turned to her dresser and glanced into the mirror. Her eyes were puffed. She made an instinctive, feminine stab at her hair before leaving the room.

Will was about to turn away when the door opened. He swung back to look at the woman and took off his hat.

"Mrs. Ross?"

She nodded in a small, stiff acknowledgment. Her glance went past Will to the two horses by the gate; it held briefly on the bay and came back to the trail boss.

"Yes?"

"I'm Will Ambers," he said.

"What can I do for you?" Her voice was uninterested.

"May I come in?"

Marilyn Ross frowned. "Mr. Ambers, I don't know you."

"I knew your husband, Mrs. Ross." Will's voice was polite.

"A great many people did." She started to close the door.

"Mrs. Ross! It's important that I talk with you."

Marilyn looked at Ambers. After a moment she nodded stiffly, stepped inside and motioned Will in.

They walked into the front room. It was small but tidy and it was furnished in the period; it showed taste, breeding and genteel poverty.

Marilyn Ross walked to the horsehair sofa and sank down on the cushions. She looked at Will without warmth.

"I'd offer you tea, but I haven't been feeling well. When you knocked I—I was lying down."

"I'm sorry if I've disturbed you, Mrs. Ross." Will settled down into a chair across from her.

She leaned toward him, her lips pursed coldly. "I'm afraid I'm not in the proper mood to welcome my husband's old friends."

"I said I knew your husband." Will cut her off. "I wasn't his friend."

He took Texas Jack's wallet from his pocket and extended it to her.

"This belonged to him; I thought you should have it."

Marilyn Ross remained seated, her body rigid. She didn't reach for the wallet.

"You must be mistaken."

Will's voice was measured; he hated having to hurt this woman. "I don't think so." He dropped the wallet on the small table next to her. "This belonged to Captain Ross, and that horse out there, the bay, and his gun."

Marilyn came quickly to her feet, her face stony and closed.

"Mr. Ambers, I don't understand you. Are you aware that my husband has been dead and buried these past five years, right here in Cottonwood Wells?"

Will's voice was grim: "Has he?"

Her lips trembled and she could not hold his gaze. But her voice was harsh.

"Mr. Ambers!"

"Your husband was alive yesterday," Will said. "He was on his way here." He paused for a moment and then said bluntly, "He was coming home, wasn't he?"

For a moment Marilyn Ross's composure cracked; her eyes had a haunted, hurt look. Then she regained control of herself.

"I don't know whom you saw yesterday," she said coldly. "Nor can I guess what you hope to gain by this, this absurd contention. My husband is buried—"

"The marshal showed me his grave, Mrs. Ross."

Marilyn bit her lip. "Then why—"

Will picked up the wallet and flipped it open. He took a faded picture from it and held it out so that she could see it.

Marilyn looked at the picture for a long moment, a knot tightening in her heart. A thousand memories crowded into her thoughts, both pleasant and bitter. But when she raised her eyes to Will her voice was flat and toneless and her face showed him nothing.

"The woman in this picture is you, isn't it, Mrs. Ross?"

"It could be."

"And these are your children?"

Marilyn nodded slowly. "Yes." Her voice was stiff, hostile. "But anyone could have—"

Will finished it for her. "Have this picture in their possession, ma'am?" Marilyn didn't say anything. Will looked closely at her. "You don't really believe that, Mrs. Ross?"

The woman turned away from him; she looked toward the door. Her voice, when she spoke, was small, but unpleasantly harsh.

"My husband went to war with that picture, Mr. Ambers. He fought through many campaigns. It could very easily have been lost, picked up by almost anyone—"

"*Was* it lost, Mrs. Ross?"

She turned back to face him.

"My husband's dead! You saw where he is buried!" She took a step toward him. "What are you after, Mr. Ambers?" She repeated it bitterly, "Just what are you after?"

Will looked into the logic of this. *Just what am I after?* He didn't know this woman; why would he want to hurt her? He had a thousand head of cattle to get through to Denver; he should be with them, minding his own business.

Yet there are some things a man must face; things that nag at him, things outside his own immediate interests. They were important, though abstractions.

Like the truth!

He answered her, choosing his words and speaking slowly, "I killed a man last night, a big man with an old saber scar over his right eye, a man with a price on his head, a man known up north as Texas Jack—"

"He wasn't my husband!"

Will made a quick gesture, cutting her off. "That wasn't his real name, Mrs. Ross; I'm sure of it. I met Captain Ross once, during the War. The man I buried on the old Comanche Trail *was* your husband!"

"No!" Marilyn's voice was sharp, almost a cry of despair. She turned away from him again, the tears welling up in her eyes.

"Please," she whispered, "whoever he was, the man you killed, let him lie out there where you buried him."

Ambers looked at her for a moment, his eyes bleak. "I wish I could," he said softly. "I wish I could."

He walked past her to the door and went out. The woman waited until she heard him ride away, then she turned, the tears streaming down her face.

"Oh, God!" she cried softly, "let him lie there—in peace."

VIII

THE LETTERING on the bank's window made an arc above Nathan Forge's head as he looked out into the drowsy square. A fly buzzed somewhere in the stillness behind him, its droning echoing a forlorn and bitter emptiness in the banker.

He had sent Marilyn Ross home and now he stood and waited, bank business forgotten. It was unimportant at the moment. He waited to see what the stranger to Cottonwood Wells would do. Nathan had never been an impatient man, but he found it hard to wait.

He and Marilyn Ross had waited five long years for this, waited in the background of their thoughts. They had known that, somehow, it would come, sometime, from somewhere.

He shifted slightly and reached to his breast pocket for a cigar. He had taken to smoking them lately, although he was a pipe man. His hand trembled and he thought, *He'll ride off; he has to! There's nothing for Will Ambers here!*

It was a prayer more than a conviction.

The monument in the square stood unchanging in the heat of the hot Texas sun. It was a dusty tribute to a man dead, to a time past, to a cause lost.

The main street ran from the square toward low, stony, hot hills. It was flanked by the buildings of Cottonwood Wells, a mixture of adobe and wood fronts in which the red-brick bank building stood out with imposing yet shabby gentility.

There was no one in the square; even the loafers had abandoned it during the heat of the afternoon and vehicular traffic was usually confined to early morning or evening.

It was a town waiting, he thought, brooding and without ambition. Its center and heart was the stone monument, in which past hopes were buried and on which its dignity now rested.

He saw the door of the marshal's office open. Jack Thomas came outside and stood on the step in front of it. The lawman looked across the square to the bank and saw Nathan Forge behind the window. Jack knew the banker, too, was waiting.

Thomas shifted slightly, his hand rubbing without conscious thought over the butt of his holstered gun. He was not a violent man, and he had lived all of his life in Cottonwood Wells; nothing beyond the horizon had ever interested him. He had his friends, and when he needed a woman, there was always Maggie's house of joy at the end of Alamo Street, past the Chinese laundry.

The stone pylon thrusting toward the brassy sky was a comfort to look at, it gave stability to the town and to Thomas. A town, like a man, needed someone to look up to.

Captain Wesley P. Ross, most decorated man in the Army of the Confederacy.

Cottonwood Wells was nothing—a shabby little town on the West Texas plains. But it would be remembered in the history books as the home of Captain Ross.

He turned now, his thoughts shifting to the rider who had appeared in the distance on the Alamo Road and a frown hardened the marshal's gaze.

Will Ambers rode toward Ross Square, Texas Jack's limping bay trailing behind, the outlaw's worn cartridge belt hooked over the bay's saddle horn, the snugged-in Colt with its silver grips reflecting the afternoon sun.

The rider and trailing horse moved like silent nemeses across the deserted square; the bay limped noticeably now, its head down almost between its legs.

Will Ambers saw Nathan Forge watching him from inside the bank and he caught the scowl on the marshal's face; he felt the hostile push of these men and there was an underlying suspicion of him in the entire town. These people wanted him gone. But he couldn't go until he found out whether the outlaw he had killed and Captain Ross were one and the same man.

A sign pointing down a side street caught his eye; "Stables" it said. He turned his horse that way, knowing he had to find rest for the bay. Will was a rancher, cows and horses were his business, and he felt a tug of sympathy for the worn-out animal.

The alley he turned into was narrow and the sun no longer penetrated there. The shadows had a welcome coolness he felt immediately. He turned into a hoof-trampled, manure-littered yard and pulled up before a big, well-kept barn.

Inside a man was forking hay into an empty stall bin. Zeke was a turkey-necked man old beyond the years when one could casually tell whether he was younger or older than his years.

He paused as he heard Will come inside leading the horses; turning, he eyed the stranger with masked hostility.

Will said, "Water and feed for both of them—two separate stalls."

The stableman came toward him, still holding the pitchfork, but there was no danger in him. He glanced at the horses.

"Overnight?"

Will considered it briefly. "I don't know . . ."

He started to reach into his pocket for money. The stableman shook his head. "Pay when you leave." He turned, walked to the bay and indicated the gun belt hanging from the saddle. "You taking this with you?"

Will said, "No . . ." and started to leave.

"Fancy gun," the man said. Then, as Will reached the doorway he said, "I won't be responsible, not for the gun."

Will looked back. "I don't expect you to." He paused. "If someone comes looking for it, let him have it. Just let me know."

He walked out and went back up the alley. He was tired and hungry, but he didn't want to stay in town longer than he had to; he knew Buck needed him.

He paused in front of the Ross Memorial. The sword imbedded in the rock was solid, like the man he had briefly known—a big man, dirty and savage-looking from the heat of battle—spurring away to take command of a battered company and turning it by sheer force of command into a fighting unit again.

The old stableman's question intruded into his thoughts and he answered for himself, because he, at least, had to know why he had come here and why he was staying.

No, I don't know how long I'll be staying in Cottonwood Wells. I only know I can't leave without knowing the truth about the man I killed.

He studied the monument again.

A stone memorial is a cold and lifeless thing; it tells very little about a man. This one said Captain Ross was a hero. Somewhere between the outlaw he had shot and the man honored here was the man he sought. Somewhere in this town was the answer to why Texas Jack, a man who had lived by his gun, had hesitated just long enough to commit suicide.

As Will started to turn away, he knew that the answer would not be found in the grave in the town's cemetery.

A burst of childish laughter suddenly echoed in the quiet square. Will looked up the street; the children were coming home from school. They poured into the square, a happy, screaming group, separating now as they headed home.

Two of them broke away from the others and came running toward Will; he had met them before.

Timmy, with his sister trailing a couple of steps behind, stopped at Will's side and pointed to the jutting saber in the stone.

"That was my pa, mister." He said it proudly, with a small boy's awe. "He was the greatest fighter in the whole world!"

Will looked past the boy to his sister. She was shyer than Timmy, but her eyes shone as brightly as she looked at the stone memorial.

They were too young to have any real memories of their father, Will thought, not if Captain Ross died five years ago. What they knew was a legend.

"Did you know my pa?" Timmy asked.

Will took a moment before nodding. "I knew him."

Susie began to tug at her brother. "Come on, Timmy. You know Ma wants us to come straight home from school."

Timmy held back. "Aw, sis, I want to talk to the man." His voice was eager. "He said he knew Pa."

Will put his hand on the boy's shoulder. "I think you better go on home," he said. His voice was firm.

Timmy looked up at him with disappointment. Then, with Susie tugging at his arm, he turned and ran off toward Alamo Road.

The three riders pulled up before the sign that indicated the way to Cottonwood Wells. Corbin dismounted and studied the recent hoof prints, then glanced up at his companions.

"We're right behind him," he said. His voice was casual, but he looked up at Lou Stillman, waiting. By unspoken agreement Lou had taken over leadership of the pursuit.

Lou glanced up at the sky. It was mid-afternoon and they could be in Cottonwood Wells in an hour without pushing their animals.

"It's been a long, long ride," Parrish murmured. "I'm glad it's ending."

Lou smiled. "Let's take a break." He waved toward a clump of trees several hundred yards off the road.

Corbin straightened, his dark face turned to Lou, his eyes questioning.

"Why wait?"

Lou was reaching inside his shirt pocket for tobacco. He shrugged. "We push him too close, he might panic. Give him a chance to settle down. If he doesn't see anyone on his back trail, he'll relax."

"Who's he?" Parrish questioned softly. At Lou's cold look, he smiled. "We don't even know what he looks like. Just who will we be looking for, Lou?"

"The man who rode into Cottonwood Wells leading Texas Jack's bay," Lou snapped. "That's all we need to know; we'll put a face on him when we get to town."

Corbin swung up into the saddle beside Lou. "Maybe he no stay," he said.

Lou looked at him. "Can the Indian talk, Corbin; it gives me a pain."

Corbin's eyes flickered with amusement or hate, it was hard to tell which.

"You're guessing he'll stay in town," he said distinctly. "You may be wrong."

Lou nodded, undisturbed by this. "We can always follow him. But I'm willing to lay odds he stays at least through the night."

He tossed his bag of tobacco to Parrish. "Come on, let's get some rest."

They turned off the road and rode toward the trees.

IX

JACK THOMAS stood in the middle of the Ross parlor. The big, awkward man faced Marilyn, his hat in his big hands, revolving it slowly between his fingers as he said uncomfortably, "I showed him the Captain's grave, Mrs. Ross. I tried to be . . . nice." It was not the word he would have ordinarily used, but he was speaking to a woman, a lady, and it was the only word he could think of. "I mean, I didn't want to give the town a bad name by beating up on a stranger. I didn't know he'd come here to bother you. I thought, once he saw where Captain Ross was buried, he'd up and leave."

Marilyn nodded. She was very tired and her eyes

were red from crying. She really hadn't wanted to see anyone, but she did not want to antagonize the man whose badge had once been pinned on by her husband.

"Mr. Ambers has come a long way out of his way to report the killing of a horse thief. He seems to be a man of conscience." She sighed softly. "He must be tired. Perhaps he'll leave in the morning."

The marshal's face hardened. "He'll leave tonight, Mrs. Ross."

She looked quickly into his face, sensing the threat there. "No," she said, frightened. "No, leave him alone. He'll go."

Thomas shook his head. "He's still going around town with that lie, ma'am."

Marilyn shrugged. "Let him." She was utterly worn out now; she did not want to argue with this man. She walked to the window and looked out. The children, she thought, would be coming home soon; she dreaded it.

Thomas watched her. He was in love with her. He had been for a long time, shortly after Captain Ross had died. But he still felt awe in her presence, and he could never be comfortable speaking to the widow of a man he and the town idolized.

He wanted to tell her that, but all he could blurt out was, "If he tries to bother you again, Mrs. Ross, I'll run him out of town!"

Marilyn's back was turned to him; her thoughts were elsewhere. But she turned the echo of what the marshal had just said, making a replay in her head.

"Thank you, Jack." She forced a smile to her lips. "But I hope that won't be necessary."

Thomas shrugged. "I can't figger it," he said, "why a man like that—trail boss, he says—would come here with a story like that." He tried to be fair to Will. "Maybe it's just an honest mistake on his part. Could be the man he shot looked like Captain Ross, maybe even called himself Ross—"

He moved toward her. "It's not an uncommon name, ma'am."

Marilyn nodded wearily. She wanted to be alone, but she couldn't bring herself to offend him.

"It's very possible, Jack." She smiled. "Thank you again for coming here." She turned to go to her bedroom. "Now, if you'll excuse me, I really have a bad headache."

The marshal forestalled her. "Marilyn!" His voice was low and urgent, and she knew that he had not come here only to tell her about Will Ambers. She turned to face him again, her face a bit strained, her smile too bright.

"Yes?"

"It's been five years now," the marshal pointed out. He took a deep breath, getting up the nerve to say what had been on his mind almost that long.

"A woman can grieve over a man only so long, even a man like Captain Ross." He paused, then began to move toward her. "I guess you know how I feel about you."

Marilyn looked at him for a long moment, judging

the determination of the man. *Oh, God!* she thought, *he repels me.*

Her voice was emotionless as she answered, "Yes, I do know, Jack. But—I'm dead, Jack—inside. I . . . I couldn't give you anything in return; it just wouldn't be fair." She closed her eyes at the look in his face. "I'm sorry."

The arrival of her children interrupted them.

Susie smiled shyly at the marshal and then went to her mother. Timmy skidded to a stop just inside the room and went into a crouch, facing Thomas; his face went play-acting hard and his right hand rose, clawing over an imaginary holster.

Thomas whirled, going along with the play . . . he made a stab for his gun, but it was too slow. He winced as if feeling the impact of a bullet as Timmy drew and shot.

Timmy cried gleefully, "Bang!"

Marilyn stepped between them, her face stern. "Timmy, how many times have I told you to stop this kind of playing?"

Timmy backed away. "Aw, Ma . . ." He turned and ran to his room, shucking his thin jacket on the way.

The marshal faced Marilyn, his face sheepish. "Just a little game, Mrs. Ross; there's no harm in it."

Marilyn looked toward Timmy's bedroom door. "Wars and guns," she said bitterly. Then, turning, she said accusingly, "No, there's no harm in it, Jack."

Thomas stood with his hat still in his hands, uncomfortable and not knowing what more to say. "I'll be back later, when you're feeling better."

She made no motion she had heard. He walked slowly to the door and looked back at her.

"I'll see that Ambers feller doesn't bother you again." He felt he had to say it. He closed the door quietly behind him. Once outside, his face hardened.

"I don't know what you're after with them lies about the Captain, mister," he muttered harshly. "But you're getting out of my town tonight!"

X

WILL AMBERS walked slowly down Alamo Road toward the square. He was hot and tired and thirsty. He thought of Buck and the cattle he was taking to Denver, and he knew he shouldn't be here, sticking his nose into something that shouldn't concern him.

He paused, looking inward on himself and wondering what it was that made a man do certain things against his own interests. Was it the way he had grown up, the way his father had pounded into him things that mattered?

"You'll be standing on your own feet some day, son, and you'll have to face yourself every day of your life.

Only thing I can tell you is: find out what matters to you, then measure up to it.

He smiled at the memory, for his father had died a failure by the judgment of his neighbors. But not by his wife's judgment, or by Will's.

He looked up now and saw that he was a few yards away from the Miner's Bar. He thought that a cold beer would help. Behind him he could feel the shadowy presence of the stone memorial; it was as though Captain Ross was watching and weighing him.

The Miner's Bar was not very big, nor was it fancy; it was just a plain saloon where men came in for a drink or a drunk, to play poker with friends or to drowse meaningless hours away.

It was, like the other establishments in town, quiet on weekdays.

Four men were playing poker at the only occupied table. One of them was Frank Simmons, a big, shaggy-haired, burly-shouldered miner. A rough man in a saloon brawl, he faced the door, the short stub of a cigar jutting from a corner of his mouth. A flat-crowned black hat sat squarely on his balding head; Simmons wore the hat indoors or out and only took it off when he went to bed.

He tossed two cards into the discard pile and reached for the deck at his elbow. He happened to look up as Will came through the doorway and he bit down hard on his cigar.

"Speak of the devil," Simmons muttered.

The others turned to look at Will. He ignored them

and walked to the bar. No one else lined the rail. The short, thin bartender had his back to Will, but he could see Will in the bar mirror. He was wiping a glass. He kept wiping it, making no move to wait on the trail boss.

Ambers waited just long enough to feel anger crawl up his spine.

"Glass of beer." His voice was quiet and controlled.

The bartender turned now, his mouth a hard, unrelenting slit. He started to shake his head.

Simmons said loudly; "Give him a beer, Rudy."

Will turned and eyed him.

Simmons pushed his chair back and got up. The man next to him said nervously, "Frank, let him be."

Simmons ignored him. He walked up to the bar and put a patronizing hand on Will's shoulder, looking at the bartender in the meantime.

"Come on, Rudy, give the great big man a beer!"

Will made no move to shrug him off. He waited, staring into the back mirror and watching the men at the poker table. Neither Simmons nor his companions were armed; or, if they were, the guns were hidden.

Rudy drew a sloppy glass of beer and banged it down in front of him.

Will reached inside his pocket, took out two bits and put it on the counter. Simmons reached out and pushed the quarter back to him.

"No charge, fella!" His voice was a challenge. "Not for the man who says he killed Captain Ross!"

The miner turned to the bartender. "What do you

say, Rudy, let's pin a medal on him. You know, the one you got laying around in that cigar box under the counter, the one the general gave you after Falls Church?"

Rudy hesitated. He knew what Simmons was playing for and he didn't want to get involved.

Will pushed his money back to the middle of the counter. He reached for his glass of beer, but Simmons thrust his big arm down in front of him, picked up the quarter and tried to stuff it into Will's shirt pocket.

"I said there was no charge, fella."

Will batted the miner's hand away. His eyes were level on Simmons now, and his voice came hard, edged with warning.

"The name's Ambers," he said distinctly. "Will Ambers!"

Simmons looked him over; his grin was dangerous. He had gained what he wanted, a rise out of the man. Now he set himself.

"Well, now, free beer ain't good enough for you in this town, *Mister* Ambers?"

Will started to turn away.

Simmons picked up the beer glass, flipping the contents into Will's face.

Will reacted, fast and violently. He hooked his right fist into Simmons stomach, just above the belt buckle and crossed his left hand in a solid smash to the side of the miner's jaw.

He hit Simmons again, with both hands, as the miner started to fold in the middle, his mouth open, trying to suck in air. The man was knocked back against the bar.

Will grabbed him by the shoulders, spun him around, put the sole of his right boot against Simmons' backside and shoved.

The burly miner went plowing into the poker table, spilling it and scattering the players.

Will braced himself against the bar, facing the miner's friends; his face was grim. Rudy made a move for the gun under the bar, but Will's cold glance changed his mind.

Simmons was on the floor, trying to catch his breath. He wagged his head from side to side, his vision blurred. He managed to turn and look toward Will; he tried to get up, but couldn't.

Ambers put his quarter down on the bar in front of Rudy.

"Beer."

The bartender drew him a glass, being very careful with it this time and set it down in front of the trail boss. Ambers drank it, not hurrying.

Then, in a dead silence, he walked out.

Two of Simmons' companions helped him to his feet. Rudy said coldly: "Somebody fetch the marshal."

XI

THE ROSS MEMORIAL seemed to mock Will Ambers as he stood on the walk in front of the bar and looked at it. Across the square, down a side street, a sign caught his eye:

SAM BRODERICK

Undertaker   Stonecutter

Nathan Forge came out of the bank as Will started to walk toward the undertaker's shop. He locked the door, and then seeing Will, he turned quickly and called.

"Mr. Ambers!"

Will turned at the banker's hail. He waited, the shadows beginning to lengthen across the square; the tip of the memorial's shadow touched him.

The banker joined him.

"I thought you had gone," Nathan said. Then, with cool candor he said, "At least I hoped you had."

"Why?"

The banker stood almost as tall as Will. In his own way he had an equal sort of stubbornness, a quiet, determined anger.

"For your own good," he said, "as well as for the peace of this town."

He waited for Will to say something, but Will just watched him grimly.

"Surely by now you must be aware of your error." The banker's voice held a trace of bitter exasperation. "I had a talk with Marshal Thomas. He assured me you'd be leaving Cottonwood Wells now that you know the truth about Captain Ross."

"The truth?" Will smiled coldly. "What is the truth, Mr. Forge? Is it here, in this town, or"—he waved—"in that grave the marshal showed me in the cemetery? Or is it in the story behind this stone monument?"

Nathan's face hardened and he made a bitter gesture. "Why, Mr. Ambers? Why do you persist in involving yourself—"

The trail boss cut in angrily, "Because I am *personally* involved, Mr. Forge!"

"Because you killed a man, Mr. Ambers?" The banker's voice held a faint skepticism. "You said he tried to steal one of your horses, that he was a man wanted by the law. You buried him. What further concern could he have been to you?"

Will pondered only briefly. "Because I couldn't leave a man, even an outlaw, to lie in an unmarked grave." He looked toward the memorial. "I'm not wrong, Mr. Forge. The man I killed I once knew as Captain Ross. His body belongs here."

He cut Nathan off with a gesture as the banker

started to speak. "All right, then, Mr. Forge, you tell me, what is the truth?"

Nathan eyed him with resentment.

"The truth is in that monument," he said. "It tells you all you need to know. Captain Wesley P. Ross, war hero, outstanding citizen, a man who—"

"Yes, Mr. Forge, I know. But what was he, as a man?"

Nathan looked across that small, quiet square; he looked back into another time and another place.

"He was the town marshal here, before Thomas came. Before the war he was a farm boy, out of Georgia." He paused and now something hard and inflexible crept into his tone. "Captain Ross died out there, on the road to the Blackjack mine, five years ago."

He turned now and made a sweeping gesture that took in most of the town.

"Not much of a place, is it, Mr. Ambers, maybe not much of a future. Just a small, dusty town on the edge of nowhere. But Cottonwood Wells has one thing no other Texas town has, something this town is proud of, something that makes a man walk tall when he crosses this square." He paused, then went on, his voice intense. "That monument—and the memory of Captain Ross!"

Will Ambers smiled cynically. "I'm sorry for you, Mr. Forge."

"Don't be!"

Nathan pointed a hard finger at the young trail boss. "Just remember this: Nothing, and no one, is going to tear down that memory."

He turned on his heel and started to walk away.

Ambers said: "Not even the truth, Mr. Forge?"

Nathan stopped and looked back. His eyes were hard. "Go away, Mr. Ambers. Ride on back to your trail herd and keep on moving. *Just leave us alone!*"

Ambers watched him walk away. He had roused hatred in a normally mild man and he pondered it briefly. What connection was there between the banker and the man the town had buried in the cemetery on the hill?

He knew he'd find the answer when he learned why Captain Ross had turned outlaw.

But it weighed on him as he turned and walked slowly toward Sam Broderick's shop.

Sam Broderick was a short, wizened man in his fifties. He was chipping away with deliberate strokes at a block of stone, using a wood mallet against the head of a stone chisel. He turned his head, a look of annoyance filtering into his watery eyes as a bell jangled in the front of the shop, but he kept on working.

He kept his undertaking and casket building confined to the shop, but he worked stone in his back yard, preferring to labor in the open. Around him were several completed headstones; the back of the weedy yard was crowded with rough blocks of granite.

Will Ambers poked his head out through the back door and surveyed the old man for a moment and then said, "You Sam Broderick?"

Sam put his mallet and chisel down and mopped sweat from his face.

"Undertaker, stonecutter, mason—any odd jobs you want done." He paused. "You looking for a headstone?"

"No."

Sam was faintly disappointed. "Eternity is a road we all come to, mister, but few of us pick the time of our going."

He walked toward Will. "What do you want?"

"You buried Captain Ross?"

The old man paused and caution tightened his mouth. He turned, went back to the block of stone and took up his mallet and chisel.

Will felt his anger rise. Since he had ridden into Cottonwood Wells he had been avoided, evaded, warned, threatened and even laughed at, and he'd had enough of it.

He crossed to the stonecutter and grabbed him roughly by the shoulders.

"Did you?"

Sam shrugged himself free; he looked back over his shoulder, his eyes flinty.

"Why are you asking?"

"Because I *have* to know!" Ambers answered grimly. *"Was* he Captain Ross?"

Sam remained silent, but his eyes avoided Will's gaze. *"Was he?"*

"His wife said he was, so did Nathan Forge." The old man's voice came harsh. "They knew the Captain better than I did."

Ambers pressed him. "But you knew him, too?"

Sam nodded. "Before he went off to war, and when he came back. Yes, I knew him."

Will was shaken by this. "Then the man you buried up on the hill five years ago *was* Captain Ross?"

"What there was of him."

The trail boss frowned. "Was of him?" Then he insisted harshly, "How did he die, Sam?"

The old man hesitated, his face hard, set in stubborn lines.

Will's voice pushed at him, bitter and angry, "Is the truth so hard to come by in this town?"

Sam reacted to the prodding. "He was killed by a shotgun blast in the face—both barrels. The Captain was on his way up to the Blackjack mine with a fifty thousand dollar payroll. He never got there."

Ambers turned and looked toward the square. "Who found him? Nathan Forge?"

Sam nodded. "Mr. Forge brought the money back to the mine and buried the Captain."

"And Mrs. Ross did the mourning?" Will's smile was wry and cynical.

"Not only Mrs. Ross!" Sam's voice was hostile now. "All of us, mister, all of us!"

Ambers eyed the old man for a long moment, seeing in the stonecutter the mood of the whole town. He walked to the back door of the shop and turned.

"Maybe it's time this town stopped mourning, Sam, and started living."

Sam shrugged. He turned and started working, chipping at the stone. He did not look back to see Will Ambers leave.

XII

FROM THE window of his room at the Mission Hotel Nathan Forge watched Will Ambers leave Sam Broderick's shop and head down the street for the stables. The room behind the banker was tastefully furnished, as luxurious as anything the town provided. It was a bachelor's room, neat and tidy, for Nathan was not a sloppy man, but devoid of feminine touches.

There were several oil paintings of seascapes on his walls; and one in particular dominated the room: a clipper ship out of New Bedford beating against the wind, rounding the Horn.

Born in a landlocked, midwestern town, Nathan had always dreamed of the sea, and it was a lasting regret that he had never stood on the shores of any sea to watch the waves beat against the rocks or the long smooth stretches of beach.

Once he had been young and footloose and there had been the opportunity, but he had stopped on his way to the Atlantic Coast to make a living; then he had been locked in by circumstance, by admiration for a man and a love for a woman. He knew he was held in the small Texas town as inevitably as if bars enclosed him.

He looked down on the square with a brooding gaze, knowing something of what was pushing the young trail boss, and yet knowing the man had to leave. Will Ambers didn't know it, but he was like a charge of dynamite; the fuse was lighted and rapidly growing shorter.

Behind him a Swiss wall clock chimed musically, reminding him it was time to keep his dinner appointment with Gabe Stockman, one of the county's ranchers. But he wasn't hungry, and he didn't feel like talking business tonight. Instead, he turned, left the room and went out to talk to Sam Broderick.

The old stonecutter was still out back, holding mallet and chisel, but he was not working. He was lost in thought, and when the front-door bell jangled he did not turn immediately. He waited until he heard Nathan open the back door.

Nathan said crisply, "Sam, you talked to him?"

Sam looked at him for a long moment before nodding.

Nathan's voice was strained as he walked to Broderick. "What did he want to know?"

"How the Captain died." The old man searched the banker's face. "Does it matter, Mr. Forge?"

Nathan stopped; his voice turned bitter. "Yes." He turned abruptly, left the shop and paused just outside to think what he felt he had to do.

His face hard, he went down the street to the Miner's Bar.

The marshal came out of the stable yard and intercepted Will on his way in. Angry, he came striding up to the trail boss.

"I've been looking for you," he said.

Will waited, his eyes bleak.

Thomas jerked his thumb back toward the stables. "Your horse is saddled and waiting for you. Now get on it and get to hell out of town!"

Unmoved, Will eyed him.

The marshal's tone became ugly. "And don't come back. Not here, not to this town!"

Will walked past him without a word and turned into the stable yard. Thomas watched him, his palm rubbing his gun butt. He seldom had trouble in town he could not handle, but he knew he was not very good with a gun and he did not want to be forced into using it.

He walked back up the alley into the square and looked at the stone shaft around which the life of the town revolved. A faint doubt crept into him.

Captain Ross was dead. His body was buried in the town cemetery. *Or was he?*

He stood there, shaken at what the possibility entailed. Then his mind closed and he *knew* Captain Ross was dead. He shut out everything else as he walked back to his office.

Will's horse was saddled and ready, as the marshal had said; even the bay was ready, tied to the saddle horn by a lead rope.

The stableman watched nervously, with a broom in his hands, as Will strode up to the animal, started to loosen the cinch straps.

His voice had no real conviction. "The marshal said—"

"I know what the marshal said!" Will snapped. "But I'll ride out of here when I'm ready and not before. Not for Mister Forge, Mrs. Ross or the marshal!"

He yanked the saddle from his horse's back and started to turn with it.

Simmons' hard voice came from behind him. "Then it'll have to be for me, trail boss!"

Will swung around to face him, still holding onto his saddle. Simmons was standing about twenty feet away. He was a man plainly intent on violence, but not wearing a gun.

"You should have stayed with your cows, trail boss. You should never have come to Cottonwood Wells."

He was moving toward Will as he talked. He stopped about ten feet away and began to unbuckle his wide leather belt. "Not come here with that lie about Captain Ross," he finished grimly.

"A man doesn't always live by what others want of him or expect of him," Will said coldly. "Captain Ross could have told you that."

The old stableman pressed back against the far wall; he wasn't part of this, and was plainly frightened by it.

Simmons began to wind the leather belt around the palm of his right hand.

"I wouldn't know about other folks," he said, "and the Captain is dead. But I know what you got coming, mister, what you've been asking for since you rode into this town."

Will dropped his saddle and moved away from it. His eyes were cold and dangerous as he looked at the heavy brass buckle dangling from Simmons' fist.

"You figure to use that on me?"

Simmons sneered. "I should have brought along a horsewhip. But this will have to do, I reckon."

"You should have brought along a gun first," Will said grimly. His hand slid down to his holster gun.

Simmons cut him off. "I have." He pointed behind the trail boss.

Will glanced over his shoulder.

Three men had come in quietly through the back door. They were Simmons' poker companions. All three had rifles. The man in the middle leveled his at Will.

Simmons' voice was flat. "Now get rid of your gun belt, cowboy!"

He was cornered, trapped. Will dropped his gun belt.

The stableman made a weak effort to stop what he saw coming.

"No . . . not in here . . ."

Simmons shoved him back. "Get out of here, Zeke. Stay out until we're through!"

Shaken, the stableman glanced at Will; then he hurried past Simmons and disappeared. Simmons twirled the heavy buckle dangling from his hand.

"No sense in waiting," he growled, and started for Ambers.

The trail boss backed up slightly as Simmons moved toward him. Simmons slashed at his face with the buckle; Will threw up his forearm and partially blocked the blow. The miner's next swing spun Will back. He stumbled over his saddle and Simmons slashed the buckle across his back.

The trail boss felt the pain of it through his entire body. He whirled and came up under Simmons' upraised hand to spin the burly miner around with a hook to the man's face. He followed this by plowing into Simmons with his head and shoulders, jamming the man up against the stall boards.

Simmons tried desperately to free his belt arm. Bleeding freely now from a cut on the side of his jaw and over his right eye, Ambers twisted the belt from the miner, spraining the man's wrist in the process. He shoved Simmons back against the boards with blind fury and held him pinned there with his left hand while he drew back with his right, ready to use the belt buckle on the miner.

He didn't see the man who came running up behind him. The man slammed the butt of his rifle against the back of Will's head. The trail boss's knees buckled and the rifleman hit him again for good measure. Will pitched forward on his face and didn't move.

One of the two other men bent over Will. "Hope you

didn't kill him, Jud." He touched the back of Will's head and looked up. He was frightened. "I didn't want a hand in murder!"

Jud, the rawboned man who had hit Will with the rifle, said, "He ain't dead. But if he was—"

"We'll have a bunch of mad drovers riding into town," the man muttered. "I've seen them wreck a town for less."

Simmons pushed away from the stall boards and looked down at Amber. The burly man was bleeding from a cut lip and his breathing was hard and fast.

"Saddle his horse!" he snarled. "And take the back way out of town; we don't want the marshal to see you. You know how Thomas feels about his badge."

The three men worked quickly. They hoisted Will's limp figure across the saddle.

"Leave him about five miles out of town, headed for the Comanche Trail. If he dies, it's his bad luck!"

XIII

THE NIGHT was soft and windless. A hundred small sounds, creeping things and chirping things, sounded in the Texas night.

There was no moon.

Parrish watched Lou Stillman pace beyond the small camp fire. Stillman was a restless man, driven by some inner torment; he never seemed to be at peace with himself. One could never be sure what Lou would do in any given circumstance. In small things he changed his mind as often as a woman.

But he had been implacable about Texas Jack and the money they had been double-crossed out of. They knew Texas Jack was dead, but Parrish knew that Lou was not yet through with him.

Parrish turned and looked at Corbin, who was lying back, dozing with his head and shoulders resting against his saddle. The half-breed moved only when he had to.

"Time to go," Parrish said softly and Corbin opened his eyes and turned to look at the pacing Stillman.

"Like lobo in cage." He glanced at Parrish. "Money mean a lot to him, huh?"

Parrish shrugged. "It's not the money."

He got up and walked to his picketed horse, carrying his saddle. Lou stopped pacing and looked at him. Parrish said quietly, "I'd like to sleep in a bed tonight, Lou. Three weeks on the trail—I've got ground sores."

Lou stared off into the night. He didn't seem to hear Parrish.

"Must have a woman in that town, Sid. He must have."

"Who?"

Lou swung around to him. "Texas Jack!" His voice held a note of cruel anticipation.

"Let's think about what we'll do when we get the

money," Parrish said. He spread his blanket over his mount's back and swung his saddle over it.

"To hell with the money," Lou said. He was looking off again, into the night.

Parrish studied Stillman for a moment. "Lou," he said softly. "I don't know about you, but I can use my share."

"We can always get more money!" Lou snapped.

This nettled Parrish. "Damn it, Lou, Texas Jack is dead! Why bother with his woman?"

Lou walked past him, not answering, and went to pick up his saddle. Corbin, coming up with his, looked back at the moody outlaw.

Parrish raised his voice. "We touch a woman in this part of the country and you'll have half of Texas on our tails!"

Corbin misinterpreted the remark. He grunted. "That why Lou pace? I get him woman. Small ranchero, just across the border—"

"That's not what Lou wants." Parrish cut him off and the half-breed looked after him, puzzled.

No one said anything more as Lou came up; they finished saddling and rode toward Cottonwood Wells, passing south of the three men riding toward the old Comanche Trail with Will's unconscious body.

They rode into Cottonwood Wells while it was still early in the evening, pausing briefly by the monument in the small square to read the inscription. The name meant nothing to them.

Most of the stores were closed, but the Miner's Bar

was open and they stopped inside for a drink. Parrish was wearing his spectacles; he appeared scholarly and despite the gun at his hip, quite harmless. Lou had put on his pleasant mood and he could look boyish when he wanted to. Corbin never changed.

There were more people in the bar now and Simmons, back at the poker table with several townsmen, was quietly getting drunk. His lip was puffed, but other than that, the miner was quite inconspicuous.

The bartender set three glasses of beer in front of them and Lou said pleasantly, "Nice town." He rubbed his stubbled chin. "We were with a trail herd going west; had a little difference of opinion with the trail boss." He grinned. "Got paid off."

The bartender's face stiffened slightly. Lou's voice was loud enough to carry to Simmons who glanced at the three men over his cards.

Parrish sipped his beer. "We're looking for a friend of ours. He said he'd wait for us here."

The bartender shot a quick look to Simmons, and Corbin shifted slowly, reaching in his pocket for tobacco; he saw the burly miner eyeing them and noted it.

"Sorry," the bartender said. "Hasn't been a stranger come to Cottonwood Wells in weeks."

Lou knew he was lying, but he shrugged. "Well, maybe he decided not to come this way after all." He finished his beer. "We've been riding a rough trail. Be good to sleep in a clean bed tonight. What do you recommend?"

"Only one hotel in town; boarding houses all full up."

The bartender waved. "The Mission Hotel, across the square."

Parrish added, "We could stand a good home-cooked meal, too." He smiled. "Any place with a good-looking waitress will do."

"Same place," the bartender answered. "Hotel dining room serves the best meal in town." He glanced at the wall clock behind him. "But you'll have to hurry. Dining room closes in a few minutes."

The three strangers went out.

Simmons got up and crossed to the bar. He looked after them and said, "They don't look like lawmen."

"Don't look like drovers, either," the bartender said.

Simmons looked at him. "You figger that feller Ambers was lying, too?"

The bartender shrugged. "Could be." He glanced toward the door. "If they're friends of his, you better get yourself a gun!"

Nathan Forge was coming out of the hotel when the three strangers walked up the stairs and went past him into the lobby. They had left their horses tied to the hitchrack. There were six horses for three men in a time when horses were still hard to come by, the war having taken most of them.

He felt a chill of apprehension and turned to look at them, but Lou, Parrish and Corbin had disappeared inside.

He started across the square on his way to see Marilyn, but was hailed by Simmons.

The miner was standing in the shadows of the Miner's Bar. He crossed quickly to the banker's side.

"See them?"

Nathan nodded.

"Said they were friends of Ambers." The miner's voice was uneasy. "Looked like gunmen to me."

"You get rid of that young trail boss?"

Simmons nodded. "Jud an' the others are dumping him off on the Comanche Trail."

Nathan eyed him; something in the miner's voice making him ask, "You didn't kill him?"

Simmons' voice was short. "He was alive when he left here."

Nathan turned and looked back to the hotel. "They could be friends of his, from that trail herd. . . ." He pondered, his eyes bitter.

"I don't want to drag the marshal into this, Frank. But if we have to—"

He motioned toward the bar. "Go back inside. I'll think of something." He smiled without conviction. "Could be they're just passing through. We'll see in the morning."

"I'm getting myself a gun," Simmons growled. "Just in case."

The banker waited on the stoop for what seemed a long time before he heard footsteps inside the Ross house and then Marilyn's frightened voice saying, "Who is it?"

He said, "Nathan," and she opened the door for him. He went inside.

The front room was vaguely lighted by a lamp, turned low. He saw she had thrown a wool wrapper over her bed clothes.

He said, "I'm sorry. I didn't know you were in bed."

"It's all right," Marilyn said. "I wasn't asleep." Her voice trembled. "I'm—afraid, Nathan . . ."

He felt a sudden surge of protectiveness for the woman; he drew her close and held her tightly, not saying anything. He could feel her crying silently, her body shuddering to release emotion.

He felt protective and responsible. Five years ago she had assented to what he had told her to do. He thought then it was the only thing to do; and he thought so now.

After a while she lifted her head to him; there were tears in her eyes.

"Nathan . . ."

"It's coming to a head," the banker said. He released her and she sank slowly down on the sofa, watching him.

"I guess I always knew it would."

"I started it all, five years ago," he said. "It's my responsibility. Whatever happens, I'll do the explaining, if we have to."

She started to say something, but he cut her off. "Three strangers just rode into town," he told her. "It may not mean anything at all. They may be just what they say they are; they could be gone by morning."

"We thought that of Will Ambers," the woman said. Her voice sounded miserable.

"He left town," Nathan said. His face didn't tell her anything more than that, although she searched it, wondering.

"Left? Why?"

"Why should he have stayed?" Nathan countered.

He put his hands gently on her shoulders, bent down and kissed her.

"Stay in the house tonight. Don't answer the door, not to anybody."

He turned to leave but she got up and followed him to the door.

"Nathan, if he's gone, then why . . ." She paused, gathering her thoughts. "Why come to tell me about the strangers? To stay locked up in the house tonight?"

"Just a precaution," he said. He avoided her eyes. "We get a visiting relative or two, a peddler, maybe a whiskey salesman, never more than one or two a month." He was silent for a moment. "Now, all in one day, four strangers show up. They're not salesmen, and they're not traveling men."

He opened the door. "Just a precaution, Marilyn." He kissed her again, gently but with feeling. "Keep your door locked."

She closed the door behind him and leaned against it, waiting until his footsteps died away. Then she bolted it and went back to her bedroom.

But she knew she wouldn't be sleeping tonight.

XIV

THE HOTEL ROOM was large by the standards of most small town hotels and it had touches not usually found in hostelries hastily hammered and carelessly sawed into shape in the frontier towns.

There were small ferns in a pot in a corner, clean window curtains and furniture that was old but hand-crafted on the east coast, in Virginia, and shipped there. There was a braided, oval rug on the floor.

Corbin spread his bedroll on the floor by the window. By preference and tacit agreement, he slept apart from Lou and Parrish. He claimed he had never gotten used to a bedspring and mattress; he liked something hard and solid under him.

None of them was getting ready to sleep.

Parrish sat on the bed, a toothpick between his teeth, and watched Lou stand in front of the mirror and comb his hair.

"The man we've been tracking is here somewhere," Lou said. "And Texas Jack's woman."

Parrish nodded. "He's here. But where?"

Lou paused, with his comb just above his hair. "All we have to do is find that worn-out bay Texas Jack rode, the one that the trail hand brought with him."

Parrish shook his head. This had always bothered him. "Why here, Lou? Why did he come here, a man with thirty thousand dollars stolen money?"

"Maybe he come to give money to woman," Corbin said. "Maybe he and Texas Jack friends."

"That's crazy!" Parrish said. He took off his spectacles and wiped them clean on the counterpane. "The man who shot Texas Jack his friend?!"

Corbin shrugged.

Lou turned. "Maybe not as crazy as you think, Sid. We don't know who killed Texas Jack. Anybody in that trail camp could have. Maybe one of the drovers recognized Jack; maybe he talked before he died. Corbin could be right. Maybe he's come here to split that money with Texas Jack's woman."

"I never go along with a man who starts his thinking with maybes!" Parrish snapped.

Lou's eyes turned cold. "All right, Sid, let's just look at the facts. Texas Jack had thirty thousand dollars of ours. He headed this way. He could have turned south a half dozen times and made it easy to the Mexican border. *But he headed this way!*"

He paused a moment. "Jack ran into this trail drive. His horse was giving out. He tried to steal one of theirs —they shot him."

He eyed Parrish. "That make sense to you?"

Parrish shrugged.

Lou continued, "We know Texas Jack had thirty thousand dollars on him. Right? Now, if them drovers didn't give a damn, they'd bury the body and divide up the money between them. Who would be the wiser?"

Parrish's smile was bleak, but tinged with a faint admiration.

"Lou, you amaze me. I didn't realize how much deductive reasoning—"

"Hell with you, Sid!" Lou snapped. "I ain't got the schooling you had, but I've got common sense—"

Corbin interjected, "Lou right. Trail hand come here."

"Let me ask you," Lou went on, ignoring the half-breed and eyeing Parrish. "Why ride to this town if you had just taken thirty thousand dollars from a dead man. Why here?"

Parrish shook his head. He didn't have an answer, but he wasn't quite convinced that Lou had.

He got up, walked to the window and looked outside. The square below was in shadows, but some stray beam of light from the Miner's Bar glinted from the hilt of the embedded saber.

Texas Jack had never talked about his past. But something stirred in the scholarly outlaw, some small recollections of the man he had ridden with not many months ago. He had been ramrod straight in his saddle; he had had a military way of organizing a raid; and he had had an old saber scar across his right eye.

He turned and looked at Lou and nodded. "Maybe you're right. Let's start by looking in the hotel stables for the bay."

Will Ambers rode back into town; hurt, he rode stiffly in the saddle, holding himself there by anger and pain.

He paused briefly in the shadows on the far side of the square and eyed the Ross Memorial for a moment before turning into the narrow street leading to the stables.

The town had quieted considerably since he had left it. All the shops had closed and even the hotel was on night shift, its dining room dark.

The Miner's Bar, however, seemed to have livened up. The voices of men mingled with the nervous laughter of the percentage girls, who, like nocturnal predators, emerged with the night.

Will rode slowly, his body racked with pain, a dull ache over his eyes. Turning into the stable yard, Zeke heard him coming. The old man stepped out, rubbing his eyes and pulling a suspender strap over his long-johns.

He stopped, jerking wide awake when he saw who the rider was. He started to back away.

Will said grimly, "Stop right there, old man!" The stableman stopped. Will brushed his hand across his bruised face. "I've got nothing against you," he said. He slid stiffly out of the saddle and hung on for a moment.

"Take good care of him for me," he said. He held out the reins of his horse.

The stableman stammered, "You can't—stay here."

The trail boss made a bleak gesture. "I don't intend to, just my horse."

The old man hesitated, then came reluctantly to take the reins from Will.

"Where can I wash?"

Zeke gestured to the horse trough by the side of the barn.

Will gave him a look, turned and walked to the trough. He pushed the scummy surface water aside, scooped up handfuls and splashed the water over his face and neck. He used his neckerchief to clean the dried blood from his cuts and then dry himself.

Watching him, the old man said, "They said you wouldn't be back."

Will faced him. With the blood washed away he felt better. But the bruises showed more plainly now and his eyes burned with a bleak savagery.

"They were wrong!"

He looked toward the barn. "That bay I left in there earlier, bring him out here, saddled just the way he was when I brought him in."

He waited as the old man went inside. He thought of Buck and the trail herd, and they seemed a thousand miles away, from another time. . . .

The stableman came out leading the bay. The animal still limped badly. Will put a hand on the animal's neck in genuine sympathy. "Sorry, feller," he muttered. "But I have to do this."

He went to where Texas Jack's cartridge belt hung from the saddle horn; the holster was empty! He swung around to Zeke. The old man backed away, whining, "I'll get it. I put it away for safekeeping."

He came back with the gun. Will snugged it tightly inside the scuffed holster.

He turned and led the tired, limping animal away.

The monument stood all alone in the square, of itself nothing, its only meaning in the hearts and egos of the people of Cottonwood Wells.

Will Ambers came into the square leading Texas Jack's bay. He led it up to the stone shaft, his face grim, his anger contained and deadly. Very deliberately he tied the worn-out animal to the hilt of Captain Ross's saber.

The bay shifted slightly. The cartridge belt hung from the saddle horn and the silver-handled gun made a small metallic sound as it hit the stone.

The memorial and the gun, Will thought cynically, *the two sides of the Captain Ross story!*

He left the bay tied there and started walking toward the Miner's Bar.

For a weekday night there was a fair crowd inside the bar. Most of the customers were at the tables, being waited on by the short-skirted girls who encouraged drinking and provided female companionship to the lonely.

The three men who had taken Ambers out of town had returned and joined Simmons. With several other miners who had come into town, they made a sizable group around a table in back.

Simmons was not worried about the trail boss; he was thinking of the three men who had just ridden into

Cottonwood Wells. He had left his companions and was now at the far end of the bar, talking to one of the girls who stood facing the door. He had a gun stuck inside the waistband of his trousers.

The girl listened, bored, but pretending lively interest. Simmons was saying: ". . . an' this ole prospector says to her, 'it warn't me who kicked yuh—it was Annie.' " He paused, a wide grin on his face, " 'Annie,' she says, 'who's Annie?' "

The girl cut in, beating him to the punch line, "And the prospector says, 'That's my jackass—' "

She broke off abruptly, eyes widening as she reacted to the appearance of Will Ambers pushing through the batwings. Simmons turned to see who had disturbed her. He jerked back; there was a startled, unbelieving look in his eyes.

Will stopped by the front of the bar. He had his gun in his hand and he looked directly at the burly miner.

"Who sent you after me?"

The girl with Simmons moved quickly away from him, joining the other entertainers who had moved to the rear of the saloon. The room had gone quiet. All eyes were on Will.

Simmons' companions sat very still in their chairs. Jud looked sick.

Simmons braced his back against the bar. He was a barroom brawler, not a gunfighter, although he could use a gun if he had to.

He watched Ambers move along the bar toward him; he felt alone and exposed in the quiet room. He needed help, but his quick glance to his companions was unrewarding.

Simmons began to sweat. He said hoarsely, "Look, feller, you wasn't supposed to come back!"

Will's voice was savage. "Who sent you?"

Simmons looked to his companions for help again, but they avoided his gaze. Desperate, he tried to stall. "We didn't mean to hurt you, fella. We only wanted to scare you, get you off our backs—"

Will cocked the hammer of his gun. It made a distinct sound, and a deadly impression on the burly miner.

"I'm asking just once more," Will said. "Who sent you?"

Simmons ran his tongue over fear-dried lips. His voice stuck in his throat.

"Nathan Forge."

The trail boss studied him for a moment, letting him sweat. "Where can I find Mr. Forge at this hour?"

"He—he lives in the hotel."

Will kept his cold and menacing gaze on Simmons. Then he turned and looked slowly and carefully at every man in the room.

"Mr. Forge better be there," he said.

He backed to the door, paused and then turned quickly and shouldered through the bat wings.

For a long moment after Will Ambers had gone no one moved.

XV

NATHAN FORGE stood by his open window, looking down on the town square. It was one of those nights when the heat of the day would linger through the early morning hours, but this was not what was keeping the banker awake.

He had turned the lamp down. It sat on the small table on the other side of the window; he cast no silhouette against the limp curtains.

He had taken off his coat and tie, the proprieties of his position no longer a necessity. He looked down on the square at the bay tied to the memorial. He studied it with the grim fatalism of a man driven into a corner and faced with only one way out.

Simmons had assured him that Will Ambers was gone and would not be coming back. He had wanted to believe that. But he had spent a lifetime studying people: he knew the losers and the winners, the quitters and those who were stubborn. It was his business to know; the bank's financial solvency depended on it.

Now more than the bank depended on his judgment. He was not surprised when he saw the trail boss ride back to town.

His brooding gaze moved across the square to the

Miner's Bar as the doors opened; he watched the trail boss step outside, turn and come striding toward the hotel.

A small, sad smile touched the banker's lips. He had not killed a man in a long time; he had never wanted to kill anyone.

But there was more than his own survival at stake. He turned away from the window and went to his closet to pick up his Winchester and a box of shells on a shelf. He had bought the gun to go hunting, but after the first year that had palled. He did not need the meat and he found little pleasure in killing for sport.

He loaded the gun with surprisingly steady fingers, considering what he was thinking.

He didn't walk back to the window; instead, he stepped out into the dimly lighted hallway and turned quickly to the back staircase.

If you have to kill a man, he thought grimly, *you didn't walk out to meet him, especially if the man was far better with a handgun than you had ever been.*

Parrish, Lou Stillman and Corbin stood in the deep shadows hiding the mouth of the hotel alley, their eyes glued to the bay tied to the memorial. They had just come from the hotel stables where they had left their horses and started looking for another.

None of them spoke, they didn't have to. They had trailed that horse more than a thousand miles, and each man knew intimately the silver-handled Colt hanging from the bay's saddle.

They waited for the man who had hitched that tired horse there.

Will didn't see them. He was crossing the square on his way to the hotel and was just abreast of the memorial when a voice hailed him:

"Ambers!"

The tone was sharp and commanding. He stopped, turning toward the voice. A shadow moved away from the marshal's office, where the window was dark. The shadow became Thomas, and he had a gun his his hand.

He walked slowly toward Will, pausing by the bay a few feet away.

The marshal indicated the animal with a jerk of his head. "You responsible for this?"

Ambers nodded. "I figured Captain Ross's bay belonged here!"

The marshal's gun hand quivered slightly as he raised it; his voice was harsh and bitter.

"You don't give up easy, do you?"

Will watched him.

"I gave you warning," Thomas said. "I wanted to be fair; a man can make a mistake—"

"I made no mistake," Will said.

Thomas stiffened. He started for Ambers. He was looking now for an excuse to kill.

"Go ahead," he rasped, "keep saying it." His gun hand steadied; the hammer cocked back. "One quick pull of this trigger—"

"And you'll bury the truth about Captain Ross! Is that what you really want, marshal?"

The three men watching from the hotel alley listened, waiting. Corbin's hand slid down to his knife; Lou stopped him. Frowning, the half-breed looked at Lou. Lou shook his head.

Parrish's gaze moved from the two men in the square to Texas Jack's horse and the stone shaft; there was a strange look in his eyes.

The marshal was quiet for a long while. "You really believe the man you killed was Captain Ross, don't you?"

The trail boss reached slowly inside his pocket. He took out Texas Jack's wallet. "I found this on the dead man."

He handed the wallet to the marshal. "There's a picture inside; take a look at it."

The lawman reached for the wallet with his left hand. He eyed Will for a moment, then slowly slid his gun back into his holster. He reached inside the wallet and took out the faded photograph. His reaction to it was gradual, a slow, gathering bitterness.

"I showed it to Mrs. Ross," Ambers said evenly. "She didn't deny it."

Thomas pocketed the photograph.

"The man you shot—what did he look like?"

"He had an old scar over his right eye," Will answered. He saw the marshal flinch slightly and he added grimly, "Captain Ross had that same scar when I saw him at Missionary Ridge."

The anger had drained out of the big lawman. He said harshly, "Why didn't you tell me this before?"

"You didn't give me the chance, like everyone else in this town." Will's voice was cold. "Remember, I was the man with the lie about Captain Ross."

Thomas looked toward the far end of town to the road that wound up the low hill to the cemetery.

"Then who *is* buried up there, in Captain Ross's grave?"

"Why don't you ask his widow?"

Thomas nodded slowly. "Come with me."

Will shook his head. "I've bothered Mrs. Ross enough." He turned away.

"Where *are* you going?"

Will looked back. "To see Nathan Forge." He touched the bruises on his face. "He didn't want me back, either."

Thomas frowned. "Nathan did that to you?"

Will's voice was thin. "Mr. Forge is a banker, marshal, he doesn't work with his hands. He just gives orders."

Thomas turned his glance to the hotel.

"If you're right, Ambers, I'll help you nail Forge." His voice hardened. "But if Mrs. Ross tells me you're wrong, I'll help Nathan kill you!"

He turned abruptly and went across the square toward Alamo Road. Will watched him for a moment, then turned to the hotel.

Lou's voice came out of the shadows of the alley next to the hotel. "Mr. Ambers!"

It was a quiet voice, rather pleasant; it carried no threat.

Will stopped at the foot of the steps and watched the

three men emerge from the shadows to come toward him. They weren't town men, he thought, and he wondered how they had come to know him; he had never seen them before.

Lou said, "Been in town long, Mr. Ambers?"

Will eyed them. Neither Lou nor Parrish with his spectacles looked particularly dangerous; he wasn't so sure about the half-breed.

He shook his head and started to go up the stairs.

Lou said: "We're strangers, too. Just got in, in fact."

Will turned, sensing something in the man's voice. It was a cold and quiet deadliness.

"That bay horse, it belong to you?" Lou waved to the bay tied to the memorial.

"No."

"Thought we heard the marshal say you tied it there."

Will stepped back onto the boardwalk, faced them. "Why are you interested?"

"We were friends of the man who owned that bay," Lou said. "Texas Jack."

Will felt a tightness crawl down his back. He waited, not saying anything.

"What happened to him?"

Will said very slowly, "I killed him."

Lou whistled softly. "You must be good with a gun, Ambers. Texas Jack was fast—"

Will cut in curtly, "I'm with a trail herd west of here. He tried to steal one of our horses."

Corbin had drifted across the square to the monument; he searched the bay's saddle bags and came back with Texas Jack's gun.

Lou gave him a look; Corbin shook his head.

Still pleasant, Lou said, "We don't care about Texas Jack, Ambers. Just give us the money."

Will felt a cold sweat on his face. He said very carefully: "Sixty cents. That's all Texas Jack had on him when—"

He stopped as Corbin moved to his side. He felt the sharp bite of the half-breed's knife against his side.

Parrish said coldly, "Texas Jack had thirty thousand dollars with him, mostly new bills, recently printed." He paused. "We don't want to make trouble here. Like Lou said, we don't care about Texas Jack. Just give us the money and we'll ride out tonight."

Will licked his lips. "I'd give it to you in a minute, if I had the money. But—"

Lou broke in, his voice suddenly harsh. "You give it to Jack's woman?"

Will looked at him, not quite sure what Lou meant. Parrish said, "Texas Jack's wife, Mrs. Captain Ross!" His smile was thin and cold. "We heard you and the marshal—Texas Jack and Captain Ross—they're the same man, aren't they?"

Ambers nodded.

Lou put a hand on his gun butt; his voice jarred, hard and impatient. "Did you?"

Will looked at them, feeling a knot tightening in his stomach. He had become a hated man in this town; he couldn't expect anyone to lift a finger for him now.

"Look," he said, "I'm telling you the truth. All Texas Jack had on him when he came to camp was sixty cents."

He pulled away from the knife at his side, his hand dipping for his gun—he paused, dry-lipped, staring into muzzle of Lou's Colt.

"He had thirty thousand dollars," Lou stated grimly. "We don't think any of the cowhands at your camp have it; we checked. That leaves you and his wife!"

Corbin slipped Will's gun from its holster and stepped back. Lou looked at Parrish.

"You and Corbin keep an eye on him." He glanced toward the lighted saloon. "Keep things quiet. From what we heard, nobody in this town'll lift a hand; he's a stranger here, just like us. And not very welcome, either."

He started to move off.

Parrish said, "Lou?"

Lou turned.

"Don't hurt her." His voice was thin. "We don't want that kind of trouble, Lou."

Lou grinned. "Just the money, Sid, just the money." But Parrish, watching him stride away, wasn't sure. He knew Lou, sometimes.

He was never sure about Lou, when it came to a woman.

XVI

THE FADED photograph lay on the small table between them, a reminder to the woman that the past somehow always manages to intrude on the present. She remembered the day all too well: the dressing of the small children; the careful attention she had paid to herself; the long minutes of waiting in the local photographer's studio while he busied himself in setting up the big box camera on his tripod, adjusting of the lens; and the seemingly eternal stiff postures before the flash went off.

This was the photograph she had sent to her husband in the last years of the War; he had kept it with him, in his wallet, ever since.

Now she looked at the woman in the photograph as though she were a stranger. The innocence and the sweetness of features belonged to another time, another woman.

The marshal's voice intruded on her thoughts. He was sad, hurt and vaguely angry. "Why, Marilyn? Why didn't you tell me?"

Marilyn Ross stood there, clutching her wool wrapper about her, her face stony, her emotions drained.

Thomas' voice was strained. "Captain Ross didn't die five years ago, did he?"

Marilyn turned away from him, her voice breaking. "No, Jack. My husband rode away from Cottonwood Wells that day with the Blackjack-mine payroll." Her voice was low, barely audible. "He left me, Jack . . . and the children. Left us to face our friends . . . the people who had looked up to us . . ."

Thomas didn't believe it at first, he couldn't. Shaken he said, "No, Marilyn! Captain Ross wouldn't do—"

She swung around to face him, bitterness harshening her drawn features. "I didn't want to believe it, either. For a long time I couldn't. But he did, Jack; he deserted me and the children. He left without even saying good-bye . . ."

Thomas turned away from the bleak despair in the woman's eyes. He walked toward the door, blindly, bumping into a corner of the sofa and not even knowing it.

Marilyn's voice stopped him; it was a small cry, lost and pleading for understanding.

"Jack—I'm sorry . . ."

The marshal turned slowly to look at her. He saw her as just a woman, down from the pedestal where he had put her and her husband. Thomas would never be quite the same again.

Held by the look in the woman's face, he stood by the door, unable to say anything. He wanted to, but his thoughts were frozen.

She went to him.

"What are you—going to do?"

He found his voice then. "I'm going to stop Ambers," he said savagely. "He's looking for Nathan. I think he wants to kill him!"

Marilyn's hand flew up to her mouth. "Oh, God, no!" Then: "Stop him, Jack! Please, stop them both."

He saw the sharp fear in her eyes, the concern for the banker, and something dark and bitter roiled up inside the big lawman.

"No," he said harshly. "Nathan asked for it. I've been a fool, looking up to you, to Captain Ross, Cottonwood Wells' little tin god . . . and all this time, you and Nathan—"

She pulled back from him, her eyes darkening. "Jack, you're wrong! It's not been that way between Nathan and me. I—"

His laughter cut her off; it had an ugly, hurt sound. "I don't give a damn, Marilyn. I just don't give a damn anymore!"

He swung around and started to leave. The knock on the door stopped him. He stepped back, looked at her, lips curling.

"Go ahead, answer it. It's probably Nathan."

Marilyn went to the door, but it opened before she reached it.

Lou Stillman stepped inside. He pushed the door shut behind him and paused as he saw the marshal; he had not expected to find the law here. He gave Jack a quick, searching glance but he did not seem disturbed, nor was his manner anything but polite.

He swept his hat from his head, held it in his left hand. He put his attention on Marilyn.

"Sorry, ma'am." He smiled pleasantly. "You are Mrs. Ross?"

She nodded numbly and glanced at the marshal.

Jack said harshly, "Who are you?"

"A friend of her—her husband," Lou replied. He had sized Jack up and knew he did not have to fear him.

"This is a poor time to come calling," the marshal said. "Let's leave whatever you have to say until tomorrow—"

He put his hand on his gun butt to back up his suggestion.

Lou said quietly, "I wouldn't do that, marshal." Jack caught the deadliness in the man's eyes and he pulled his hand away.

Marilyn made a gesture toward the bedrooms. "My children are asleep, and my husband is dead. Surely, some other time—"

"It's just a matter of money," Lou said.

She shot a frightened look at Jack.

The marshal said, "What money?"

"Thirty thousand dollars." Lou turned his gaze back to the woman. "You must have known. He was on his way here with it."

She shook her head. "I'm afraid I don't understand. My husband's dead."

"He is now." Lou smiled. "But I knew him when he was Texas Jack, rode with him more than three years."

She backed away a bit and turned her eyes to the marshal, pleading.

Thomas moved close to Lou. "I think you've made a mistake," he said. His voice roughened. "Now get out—"

Lou's right hand moved faster than Thomas could see; he felt the hard muzzle prod his stomach and he shrank from it, fear licking up into his eyes.

Lou put his hat back on his head; he reached out, lifted the marshal's gun from his holster and tossed it on the sofa.

He was no longer pleasant.

"Turn around," he said coldly. "Stand three feet from that wall." He waited until Thomas obeyed. "Now put your hands against the wall and stay that way!"

Jack hesitated just a moment . . . he looked at Marilyn, at Lou; then he leaned forward and braced himself against the wall.

Lou turned his attention to Marilyn.

"I always figgered Texas Jack had a woman somewhere. Used to see him look at a photograph he had— nights, mostly, around a camp fire. But he was a close-mouthed man, ma'am; he never said."

Thomas shifted slightly and Lou shot a look at him. The marshal was sweating.

"Never figgered Texas Jack for a military man, a captain." Lou still found it hard to believe. "Is it true, marshal, he was a hero in the war?"

Jack didn't say anything.

Lou turned back to Marilyn.

"We got the man who killed him, ma'am. He said he

didn't find any money on Texas Jack." He walked up to her and she shrank from him, stopping only when she backed into the sofa.

"Leaves only two ways to figger it," Lou said coldly. "Ambers is lying, or Texas Jack got the money to you, some way."

Marilyn said stonily, "I don't know what you're talking about."

Lou slapped her, hard.

The marshal pushed away from the wall, but froze as Lou's gun swung around to him.

"I ain't ever had much patience with women," Lou said. "Ain't any of them can talk straight an' honest when it comes to answering a simple question."

He reached out, swung her roughly around the sofa and jammed her down into a straight-backed chair. He held his gun loosely by his side, but its threat was there.

"Now, about that money—?"

Marilyn was terrified. Thomas remained with his palms braced against the wall, sweating, locked in an agony of conflicting emotions. This was the first time he had run up against a man who sent fear crawling through him; Jack was not a timid man.

"I don't know anything about any money my husband may have had," Marilyn said. She shrank back against the chair as Lou cocked his gun.

"Oh, God!" she moaned, "how can I tell you what I don't know!"

"Mommy!"

The cry came from Timmy's bedroom doorway. Lou

spun around and paused as he saw the boy, rubbing his eyes, still half asleep.

"Mommy, who's that?"

Marilyn half rose, then settled back as Lou eyed her. "Timmy, go back to bed!" Fear choked her voice.

Timmy looked at Lou and at the gun in his hand. He smiled. "Hey, I'll get my gun—"

He disappeared inside the bedroom. His eyes narrowing, Lou took a step after him.

Marilyn sprang from the chair, her voice rising, hysterically. "No, no—you don't understand!"

She went for the outlaw; Lou turned and backhanded her across the face. She stumbled and fell across the small table.

Timmy appeared in his bedroom doorway with a gun in his hand.

Thomas broke away from the wall and dived for his gun on the sofa. He got his fingers around it and straightened. Lou shot him.

The lawman staggered, dropped his gun and went to his knees. His eyes glared at Lou. "Kid—toy gun—don't shoot—"

He sagged forward and went still.

Marilyn staggered to the side of her son, who was staring at Thomas, his eyes wide, not wholly comprehending.

Marilyn whimpered: "Timmy, Timmy . . ." She took the gun from him and threw it blindly behind her. She stood in front of him, shielding him and facing Lou.

Lou walked over to the toy gun, kicking it aside. He said ironically, "Shouldn't let kids have guns, ma'am."

Susan appeared behind Timmy, rubbing her eyes. "Mommy, what's that noise?"

Marilyn pulled her close behind her. She looked at Lou; her eyes were dark and tortured. "I don't have much money. But I'll give you everything I have. Just—just leave us alone."

Lou considered.

"That trail boss, Ambers, he came to see you, didn't he?"

She nodded.

"What did he want?"

"He said he had killed a man who had tried to steal one of their horses. He thought—it was my husband."

"Captain Ross?"

She nodded again.

"He didn't have any money with him, didn't say anything about money he found on your husband?"

She shook her head.

Lou frowned. It was just possible, he thought, Texas Jack had outfoxed him and hidden the money somewhere along the long run to Texas, maybe intending to return to pick it up later.

Frustration backed up in him like gall and he said, "Your husband owes me thirty thousand dollars. Your life worth that much, Mrs. Ross?"

She shrank from the look in his eyes.

"I told you, I don't have much money. I have two children to support; I work in the bank for a living."

Lou's eyes glittered.

"Who's your boss?"

"Nath—Mr. Forge."

Lou smiled. "Nathan, eh? You sound like he's more than your boss, Mrs. Ross."

She closed her eyes, her lips trembling.

"Your life worth that much to him, Mrs. Ross?"

She shook her head, her eyes still closed.

"Look at me!" he said sharply. He pointed to the children as her eyes opened. "What about them? How much are they worth to you—and Mr. Forge?"

Her voice was choked. "Nathan doesn't have that much money."

"The bank has!"

Lou motioned with his gun. "Put them back to bed. I'll wait for you."

She stood still, numbed by the enormity of this. She looked at Thomas, lying still on the floor by the sofa. He was breathing; he was still alive, but that was all she could tell.

"I'll give you two minutes!" Lou snapped.

She knew, as she turned with the children into the bedroom, that he would not wait one minute more.

XVII

Texas Jack's horse shifted slightly, his hind legs spread wide. A shiver went through him; the great heart that had carried him and his rider over a thousand miles of trail was giving out. He turned his head and looked at the three men by the monument.

Corbin was hunkered down by the base of the shaft, Will's gun thrust into his waistband. He was holding the silver-handled Colt he had taken from the bay's saddle and examining the crossed sabers etched into the butt plates.

He glanced at the horse, his face impassive.

Parrish leaned against the memorial. He kept his hand near his gun, but he seemed relaxed. Will Ambers stood a few feet away.

The three of them made a small group by the stone monument. They looked friendly, like three men having a little chat in the square.

Parrish said, "Goes to show you, Ambers, you never can tell about a man." He glanced at the saber handle jutting from the stone. "I rode with Texas Jack three years and never even knew he fought in the War."

Will looked past the monument. The town was quiet,

most of its inhabitants asleep. Only the Miner's Bar lights were still on, but most of the men who had been inside earlier had left. He had seen them leave, singly and in pairs, throwing curious glances in their direction.

He had not seen Frank Simmons emerge, but it mattered little to Will; the miner would have no interest in what happened to him.

He looked at Parrish. "Mind if I smoke?"

Parrish shrugged.

Will reached inside his shirt pocket and took out his sack of tobacco and papers.

Corbin glanced down the dark Alamo Road. They had heard a shot a few minutes before, but it was muffled and then it was quiet. Neither he nor Parrish had shown much interest.

But Will remembered that the marshal had gone to the Ross house.

Parrish read the inscription on the face of the stone monument.

"This town must have thought a lot of Texas Jack," he mused. He looked at Will, who was lighting up. "You knew him?"

Will nodded. "Most decorated man in the Army of the Confederacy," he said, "when I knew him."

Parrish smiled. "Never took sides, myself." He glanced down the street. "Lou did. Still hates the North."

Corbin shifted slightly and drew a line in the dirt at his feet. "We get money, we leave tonight?" He looked at Parrish. "Long way to Mexico."

Parrish nodded. "We leave tonight."

Simmons walked slowly to the doors of the saloon and glanced out at the three shadowy figures in the square. Only a few men remained in the bar; the girls, sensing things were not right, had retired to their rooms.

He turned and looked back to the bartender. "They're out there, waiting for somebody," he said. "Talking friendly as you please."

One of the men at the miner's table said, "Maybe they'll go away." It was a wish shared by all of them.

The bartender was worried. "Somebody ought to tell Thomas and warn Mr. Forge."

Simmons stopped by the bar. "Can't understand it; when that trail boss left here he was headed for the hotel."

He looked at the few men left at the table. None of them moved.

He said, "I'll get Thomas."

The bartender motioned to the back door. The miner nodded; he went out that way.

He came up behind the law office; the back door was locked. He moved around to the side window, but it was dark inside and he guessed that Thomas had closed up for the night.

Simmons paused. He didn't want to go around to the front where he could be seen by the men in the square. He thought for a moment. Thomas stayed at the Caswell Boarding House, but it occurred to him that Thomas could do little about the men in the square. They were not bothering anyone.

A shadow moved behind him and he heard the foot-

step before he whirled, his mouth dry, his hand going
to his gun.

"Hold it, Frank!"

Nathan's voice cut at him. Simmons let out a relieved
breath and waited as the banker came up beside him.
The banker was carrying a rifle and even in the faint
light the miner could see the change in the man.

"What you doing out here?" Nathan asked.

"Looking for the marshal." Simmons made a gesture.
"I was going to go by the hotel, to wake you."

Nathan frowned. He had an idea where the marshal
might have gone.

"That trail boss, Ambers—he's back," the miner said.
"I know."

"He's looking for you." The miner's voice was low. "At
least, he was when he left the bar. Now—"

Nathan gestured toward the square. "What's going on
out there?"

"I don't know." Simmons knuckled his jaw. "There was
three of them came into the bar earlier, said they were
friends of Ambers. When that trail boss came back, they
joined up with him in front of the hotel. Then one of
them left and went down Alamo Road, walking."

A stab of apprehension went through the banker. "Just
one of them? You sure?"

Simmons nodded. "You think he went to Mrs. Ross's
house?"

The banker said, "I'll find out!" His voice was grim.

Simmons fingered his gun. His voice was not con-
vincing. "Maybe I better go along—"

"No!" Nathan gestured toward the bar. "Go back and wait. I'll handle this."

The miner looked toward the square. "Three of them, Mr. Forge?"

"I'll get Thomas," Nathan said. "Go on back to the bar. No sense in you getting involved, maybe hurt."

He moved away in the darkness before the miner could speak.

The Ross house had a dim light burning in the front window; the big tree in the yard shadowed it. The dog-house lay beyond it.

Nathan moved silently toward the gate, his rifle held across his waist, ready to fire. It had been a long time since the War, but the years were slipping away now; he moved without hesitation, alert and ready to kill.

A shadow moved across the lighted window and a moment later the door opened. He saw Marilyn pause in the doorway; she had put on a dress over her night-clothes, nothing more.

Then a man's figure loomed up behind her. It was a tall, lean man Nathan knew instantly was not the marshal.

Lou's voice drifted to him. "We'll take it easy, ma'am. No hurry. We don't want to alarm the neighbors, do we?"

Marilyn started down the steps. Lou closed the door behind him. They walked toward the gate, Lou a couple of paces behind her; both were little more than shadows.

The dog in the little house past the tree came to the opening and looked out at them; he was the sort of dog that barked excitedly during the day but remained silent at night. Mrs. Ross had not encouraged him to do otherwise.

Nathan waited, tense, his eyes bright. He knew the man walking behind the woman would not hesitate to shoot her. What he had to do would have to be fast and accurate.

He waited until Marilyn reached the gate and dropped her hand to the latch. Lou paused a few feet behind.

Nathan said sharply: "Marilyn—*move!*"

She froze instead. The banker shot past her, his nerves taut as Lou reacted instantly. His bullet knocked the outlaw back against the trunk of the tree. His hand came up with his gun just as Nathan shot him again; he slid sideways and fell into the deeper shadows.

The dog began to bark; it was half whimper.

Marilyn started to sag as Nathan reached her and took her in his arms.

"It's all right," he breathed. "It's all right. . . ."

He looked past her to the house. "What happened to Thomas?"

She clutched at him, crying softly. She did not answer for a few moments.

The dog ceased barking; he remained in the opening, whimpering.

Finally she said, "He . . . he shot Jack . . ."

Nathan shot a look up the dark street. He knew the shots would be heard by the men in the square.

"Get back inside and bolt the door!"

She clutched at him. "Thomas—he may be dying . . ."

"For God's sake, Marilyn!" he said harshly. "The others will be coming any time. Get inside; *bolt the door!*"

She looked into his grim face, not recognizing him as the soft-spoken banker she worked for.

"Nathan . . ."

He pushed her back toward the door. "Don't worry about me."

She backed off, glanced at the barely discernible body under the tree. Her eyes closed. She turned and ran into the house.

Nathan waited until he heard her lock the door. Then he shot a glance up the street.

Surprise was a potent weapon, as was the willingness to kill.

He moved quickly into the shadows behind the house.

XVIII

Sid Parrish pulled away from the stone shaft and stared toward Alamo Road, the rifle shots echoing disturbingly in his brain.

Corbin straightened and looked at him, his button-black eyes glittering.

"Lou, he run into trouble."

Parrish said tightly, "Maybe." He glanced at Will. "I'd better go check."

Corbin said, "What we do with him?"

Parrish thought a moment. "Lou wanted him here . . . and you know how Lou is."

Corbin shrugged.

"Give me five minutes," Parrish continued. "If you hear more shots and Lou and I don't come back, kill him!"

Corbin watched him cross the square. He looked at Will then, his voice laconic.

"You give me money, I let you go."

Ambers eyed him. *Is the half-breed serious?*

"You have the money?"

Ambers made a small gesture. "It's my money now." *I have nothing to lose*, he thought grimly.

Corbin shrugged. "Half for you."

"What about them, your partners?"

Corbin was emptying Texas Jack's gun; he slid the shells into his pocket.

"I mostly Indian. I get old; who think about me then?" He dropped his right hand to his knife. His eyes studied Will. "Half the money?"

Will said, "They'll follow us."

Corbin slid his knife out and ran the edge slowly across the corner of the stone memorial.

"They no find me. You?" He raised his shoulders slightly.

Ambers said, "I hid the money just outside of town near the schoolhouse."

Corbin nodded. "We walk."

"Faster if we rode."

Corbin eyed him, unwinking. "We walk."

Ambers hesitated.

Corbin tossed him Texas Jack's empty gun. "I give you bullets when we find money."

Ambers hefted the gun. The Indian played a good poker hand, but he was not unreadable. Ambers knew this was Corbin's idea of finding the money. He'd shoot Ambers immediately, whether they found it or not.

He turned as if to cross the square. He saw Corbin come up behind him as he moved past Texas Jack's horse. Will whirled, jamming his shoulder against the animal's hindquarters.

The bay staggered into the half-breed as Corbin flipped his deadly knife; the blade scraped the top of Will's shoulder.

Will kept moving. He plunged into the half-breed as Corbin went for the gun in his waistband. He rammed his shoulder into the man, jamming him back against the sharp corner of the memorial.

Corbin grunted, his face twisting in pain. Ambers clubbed him with Texas Jack's Colt; he struck him again as the outlaw went down.

He might have killed him. Will didn't know. At any rate, Corbin would not be getting around for a while.

He took his gun from the unconscious man and glanced at the saloon. He thought of Marilyn Ross. He started at a run toward Alamo Road.

Will heard the rifle shot while he was still a hundred yards from the Ross house. He stopped abruptly. *Just one shot!* He waited, but there was no other sound except a small dog whimpering.

Will glanced around him. The surrounding houses were dark. The people inside must have heard the shots, but no one was about to interfere.

There was a smell of fear all up and down the darkened road.

He moved cautiously, coming to the Ross gate. There he found Parrish, lying just inside. His gun was clutched in his hand; he had never gotten to fire it.

Will looked at the house. There was a dim light against the window.

He thought it was inconceivable that Mrs. Ross would have shot Parrish.

He moved inside the gate and paused part way up the walk. He called; "Mrs. Ross!"

The house was quiet. He thought he caught a glimpse of someone at the window. He started toward the door, his gaze shifting, searching the shadows.

He saw another body under the tree; somehow he knew it was Lou, even before he crouched down and turned the outlaw over.

Lou was dead. So was Parrish.

Who?

Nathan's voice answered him from the shadows alongside the house.

"Drop your gun, Ambers! Move away from it!"

Ambers dropped the gun and moved back toward the small front walk.

Nathan came out of the shadows, holding his rifle.

Will eyed the grim-faced man coming toward him. He was not the soft-spoken banker he had talked to earlier.

"You killed him?"

"Both of them." Nathan's voice was hard and without regret.

"And you're going to kill me, too?"

Nathan paused; he nodded slowly.

Will's voice was bitter. "Is it worth that much to you, this thing you're hiding about Captain Ross? Worth enough for you to kill me for it?"

Nathan's voice was strained. "Yes." He took a deep breath. "I didn't want it to come to this, Ambers. I had enough of killing in the War; I never wanted to kill again."

Will glanced at Lou's body in the shadows.

"Killing can get to be a habit, Mr. Forge, like it did with Captain Ross."

The banker nodded; his voice was slow and bitter. "Yes . . . like Captain Ross . . ." He glanced toward the house. "For him it *was* the War and the medals! He never got over it, never regained his balance, his sense of values." His voice harshened. "But what he was before is what matters—*the only thing that matters!*"

The trail boss measured his chances against that leveled muzzle. Sweat beaded around his lips.

Dry-mouthed, he said, "Is it? Or is it your own skin you're concerned with? Your own guilt?"

Nathan eyed him, smiling wryly. "*My* guilt, Ambers?" He shook his head. "I never valued my skin that much."

He shifted his rifle muzzle slightly; it was leveled at Will's chest.

"There are some things a man will kill for, some things more important than himself."

Ambers tensed. "Even more important then the truth?"

Nathan shrugged grimly. "I could have killed you a half-dozen times from my window. But I kept hoping you'd go away and leave us alone."

His finger started to tighten on the trigger of his rifle. "Now you've given me no choice."

"*Nathan!*"

The banker twisted to face the house, but he kept an eye on Ambers.

The marshal leaned in the doorway, a gun in his hand and his back against the jamb. He looked very tired, badly hurt. But his voice was steady enough as he said, "Drop the rifle, Nathan!"

Nathan eyed the lawman and the woman standing just behind him.

He said defiantly, "Jack, I can still put a bullet in him before you pull that trigger."

Marilyn pushed past the marshal and ran down the steps. She stopped between Will and the banker.

"Nathan!" she cried brokenly. "I told Jack—the truth!"

Nathan stared at her, his shoulders slumping. She turned to face the trail boss.

"Yes, it *was* my husband you shot, Mr. Ambers! My husband who deserted me five years ago . . ."

Nathan said, "Marilyn, no . . ."

Marilyn ignored him.

"I've always been a proud woman, proud of myself, proud of my husband, my children." Her voice broke and she was silent for a moment. Then she said, "But he left me."

She turned to the banker, her voice softening. "Tell him, Nathan—Jack, too. Tell them the truth."

Nathan shook his head.

Marilyn turned and looked at the marshal in the doorway; then she turned to Ambers.

What Nathan did was for all of us!

The marshal intruded, his voice low and bitter. "I always thought Captain Ross died saving the Blackjack payroll."

Marilyn shook her head. "No. My husband took the payroll and rode off with it." She paused, looking at Nathan. *"Tell them, Nathan."*

The rifle in Nathan's hand lowered as though it had become a weight too heavy to hold. He looked at Marilyn. All that he'd done was primarily for her, and he'd do it again, if he could.

His voice was flat, almost emotionless. "Ross was taking the payroll to the mine that day. A drifter tried to hold him up." He paused; it still was not an easy story to tell.

"I was waiting for Ross at the mine. When he didn't show up I went after him. I found the drifter's body on the trail. The payroll and Ross were gone." He shrugged. "I knew then what had happened. I guess I had known Ross was just waiting for a chance like this."

A flash of emotion crossed his face. "May God forgive me, I used a shotgun on the drifter!"

In the doorway Thomas slowly lowered his gun; a look of pain crossed his face.

"Captain Ross had been my friend, and I knew what made him do this. I couldn't let him destroy all those who had believed in him—make a mockery of that monument in the square."

He was looking at Thomas now, speaking to him. "The mine would have shut down without that payroll, Jack. So I took the money from the bank and made up the loss—"

Marilyn cut in, her voice gentle.

"Nathan's been juggling the books for five years, putting that money back, a little at a time—"

Thomas cut in on her: "Then you really buried an unknown drifter in Captain Ross's grave?"

"We buried the spirit of Captain Ross in our cemetery," Nathan replied, "the soul of the man all Cottonwood Wells knew and loved . . ."

"And then lived under the shadow of his return for five years?" Will shook his head slowly.

Marilyn nodded. "Five long years, Mr. Ambers." She walked to the banker's side and turned.

"Nathan tried to spare me the truth, but my husband was less kind. Two months after I thought I had buried him, I received a letter with no return address postmarked somewhere in Nebraska." Her smile revealed her hurt. "He must still have had some residue of conscience. He wrote to tell me where he had hidden twenty thousand dollars of the payroll. I was to use it to live on . . ."

Ambers frowned. He glanced at Lou's body. "Is that the money he—"

"No." Marilyn's voice was firm. "It couldn't be." She looked at Thomas. "It was the bank's money. Long ago I turned it over to Nathan."

She turned back to face Will. "The money that man talked about, thirty thousand dollars, I know nothing about. Believe me, Mr. Ambers, I know nothing about it."

"Neither do I," Will said. He took a breath. "If he had that kind of money, and I think now he did, he must have hidden it before I met him."

He moved to his gun and picked it up.

Nathan said: "Ambers!" and the trail boss looked at him, his eyes cold.

"You wanted to know the truth," Nathan said bitterly. "But is the truth better than the lie? For Captain Ross's children? For this town? For all the folks who believed in him?"

Will considered this; he had found out what he had come here for; he would no longer be tormented by doubt.

He shook his head.

"It's your lie," he said, "and you'll have to live with it. You and Mrs. Ross, and—"

Will put his gaze squarely on the marshal.

Thomas took a long time answering. "As far as I'm

concerned Captain Ross is still buried here in Cottonwood Wells."

Will holstered his gun. "I left one of them lying by the monument. I don't know if I killed him. But he knows about Captain Ross, some of it, anyway."

Thomas said, "I'll see that he doesn't talk. I'll put it to him: ride out of town, or hang!"

Will smiled.

"I'll ride out now, Marshal, if it's all right with you."

Thomas nodded slowly.

The letter came a day later, postmarked somewhere in Colorado, no return address. It was delivered to Marilyn Ross at the bank; she opened it with trembling fingers.

It was from her husband, and it said simply that he was coming home.

She looked at Nathan. "I wonder what he did with the money they said he had?"

Nathan shrugged. "We'll never know."

They never did. But Texas Jack, a man with a bad heart coming home to die, had returned the money to the company from which it had been stolen.

The holdup had been his idea, and then he'd had a change of heart. He knew Lou, Parrish and Corbin would never believe it.

He didn't think it important enough to write his wife.

They were waiting for Will Ambers at the river, as Buck had said they would. The herd was scattered along the grassy bank, the horses were resting.

Buck said, "How'd it go?"

Will shrugged.

Buck eyed the bruises on the trail boss's face. "Was he Captain Ross?"

Will eyed him. "That's a hell of a thing to ask, with a thousand miles of trail ahead of us."

He spurred off.

Buck looked after him for a moment, scowling. He knew Ambers. He'd tell him, when he was ready.

It took two shots to get the Ranger from ambush. The first one spun him around. The second dropped him. He lay still as the life ebbed out of his body.

The *Amigos*, a group of Mexican revolutionaries, was being used as a front for Cass Borman's slick rustling operation. Borman's gang was made up of the worst killers on either side of the border. But into this group came someone new. He was young, lean, hard.

Pete Galahad, he called himself. They tried to bully him—at first. Then they became a little afraid of him. There was something of the smell of death about him.

And then, one day, there was a showdown. In the split second it took Pete Galahad to draw his gun, he gazed into the eyes of his brother's killer.

Turn this book over for
second complete novel

The
DEADLY
AMIGOS

BARRY CORD

AN ACE BOOK

Ace Publishing Corporation
1120 Avenue of the Americas
New York, N.Y. 10036

I

FROM WHERE the Mexican woman stood frozen against the crumbly adobe wall enclosing the well, she could see the butte around which the trail to the border town of Candelaria curled like some dry snake. She could see it if she raised her eyes, but Juanita Malinas was staring with numbed fear at the slim, insolent-faced man inside the doorway of her *jacal*.

He was holding Ramirez, her ten-year-old boy, one hand clapped to his mouth. The other hand held the razor-sharp blade of a hunting knife lightly against the unmoving boy's throat.

"You do as I say!" the man hissed. "Scream when he is close enough for him to hear you—or your *muchacho* will never again run after the goats!"

The Mexican woman nodded mutely. She was a dumpy, shapeless widow eking out a bare living running goats and selling milk and cheese in town once a week. A widow too poor to attract even a petty thief, she still could not comprehend the calamity which had befallen her.

The two men had ridden up to the *jacal* an hour ago, had taken possession of the place and waited until

5

the dust banner under the distant butte indicated that a rider was heading this way.

Now she stared, still not fully understanding, but knowing only that her only son, her comfort and reason for living, stood within a hair of death.

The man holding Ramirez was slim, young and burned dark as Juanita. But he wasn't Mexican. His hair was sandy, streaked by the border sun, and his eyes were gray and stood out against the darkness of his cheeks.

The other one who had led the two saddle horses out of sight behind the goat shed was an Indian—a Yaqui, sullen and stolid and as broad as he was tall. A bandolier crossed one thick shoulder. The carbine he held in his hands was an old German make, a single shot Krag.

The man in the doorway could not see the road, only the woman by the well. But his voice held an ugly threat. "Make sure he hears—"

He broke off, listening. The sound of an iron-shod animal on the hard-baked road reached him in the buzzing stillness. His face tightened. "Now!" he whispered harshly and made a quick motion with his knife.

Juanita screamed. There was real terror in it, shattering the hot afternoon stillness.

Jeff Corrin was on his way to a rendezvous with his brother in Candelaria. But when he heard that scream he instinctively jerked his horse toward the *jacal* baking on the desert flat. Against the vast emptiness of the border wilderness the *jacal* had been hardly discernible and he'd paid no attention to it.

Now he saw the woman standing by the well, holding her hands to the sides of her face. She kept screaming. . . .

The ex-Ranger's eyes made a quick survey of the yard, noting nothing amiss. But something must be wrong, he thought, for this woman to scream with such agonizing terror.

He rode into the yard and pulled up a few feet away. The woman did not look at him, nor did she quit screaming until he slid out of saddle. Jeff's horse stood between him and the door of the adobe hut.

"*Señora,*" he said quickly. "What is wrong?"

The woman had ceased screaming. She stood against the well lip, her eyes closed. Her mouth seemed working in silent prayer. Then she made a motion with her hand, into the well.

"My boy, *señor* . . . he fell. . . ."

Jeff moved toward her, concern quickening his step. "I'll take a look—"

He saw her eyes open and fix on the door behind him and a warning rang sharply in Jeff Corrin's head. A mother who had just seen her son fall into a well would be more frantic, more concerned with the boy's immediate plight . . .

His big steeldust snorted warningly. Many times in the past the stallion's keen senses had alerted Corrin to hidden danger . . . he reacted now to the animal's warning with the quickness of a jungle cat.

He spun around just as a small boy hurtled out of the doorway to fall on his face in the yard . . . and

then he caught the glitter of sunlight from the knife as it spun toward him.

Jeff's gun was already nestling in his right hand as he turned; he fired once at the knife and it disappeared. His second shot caught the slim gunman dragging at his holster gun.

The man screamed and fell back inside the *jacal*. The woman broke away from the well and fell across her son who lay quiet, sobbing loudly.

From the shed a carbine blasted heavily. The slug chipped adobe from the well rim, screamed wildly off into the desert emptiness.

Jeff caught sight of the squat Yaqui just before the man ducked behind the shed. He made a run for the flimsy structure, skirting the well. A goat, frightened by the gunfire, lunged against its tethering rope, bleating with terror.

Horses blew heavily. Jeff was just rounding the shed when they broke away, stirrups flapping, kicking up dust in wild flight.

The Yaqui almost caught Corrin with that trick.

But the fleeing horses caught Jeff's attention and he stopped, and only the blur of movement along the base of the shed saved him. He lunged aside and ducked and the reloaded Krag air-whipped a bullet past him; then his own Colt emptied in a staccatto burst.

The Indian twisted like a headless rattler; he dragged himself a few feet along the shed before collapsing.

Jeff walked up to him and eyed the still figure. Nobody he'd ever seen before. The silence held only

the bleating of the goat and the softer sobbing of the frightened boy.

Jeff walked back to the yard. The woman was on her knees now, holding the boy to her and rocking him gently.

Jeff waited, his narrowed gaze studying the dismal scene: A squalid Mexican *jacal* in the middle of a lonely desert plateau. Two men he had never seen before waiting to kill him.

He knew that this woman and her son had been nothing more than bait to bring him here; he understood the reason for this, too. For at least twenty miles along the trail he had come there was no place where an ambusher could have concealed himself close enough to insure his mission.

He knew this, but not the reason for the ambush. Unless it had to do with his brother, waiting for him in Candelaria.

But no one was supposed to know that he was to meet Texas Ranger Ben Corrin in Candelaria today. No one except Ben.

He bent over the woman and put a gentle hand on her shoulder.

"Is the boy hurt?"

There was something in Jeff's voice that drew the woman's attention. She looked up, her leathery features still frozen in a mask of fear.

She saw a young man, sun-browned and blue-eyed, standing over her—a lean, quietly smiling man with a dimple in the middle of his chin and a strange glint

of recklessness in his gaze. He was dressed no differently from the killer who had held a knife to her son's throat, but she saw the sympathy in his face and she reacted to it.

"They made me do it, *señor*. They came an hour ago. Ramirez was with the goats. They brought him to me." She shook her head, not comprehending. "I am a poor widow—I have nothing. I told them. They said they wanted nothing of me. They said they would give me fifty pesos if I did what they wanted. I was to scream when you rode by . . ."

Jeff nodded. "Well, it's over," he said as the woman started to sob again. "No more harm can come to your boy."

He walked to the *jacal* and looked down at the dead man. He looked like some range rider who had just taken off his chaps and come to town for a few drinks. Two fancy, pearl-handled guns in tooled leather holsters were the only odd note; most punchers couldn't afford belt and guns like that.

A tough-looking American and a Yaqui border thief; they made an odd combination. They didn't make sense, either, he reflected—unless they belonged to the outfit that was stirring up all that trouble in Chihuahua.

Jeff thought of his brother waiting for him in Ansara, a whistle stop flanking the tracks of the El Paso & Chihuahua Railroad Line.

He bent and, struggling, picked up the dead man and carried the body behind the shed where he dropped

10

it beside its companion. Then Jeff walked back to Juanita.

"I'll see that someone in Ansara is notified," he told her. "Someone will come for the bodies and bury them." He touched the brim of his hat to her. "*Buenas dias, señora.* . . ."

The big horse snorted as he mounted. He turned the stallion away from the *jacal,* put it to a run toward the down below the distant rim.

His brother was waiting for him in Ansara. But Jeff had the ominous feeling that Ben already was in trouble.

II

"You ARE waiting for someone, *señor.* I see it here, in the way the sand lies . . ."

She was an old crone, a bag of bones rattling inside a brown, wrinkled skin. Her eyes were black shoe buttons, peering through brown paper lids.

Ranger Ben Corrin's big square hand rested on the table in the cantina. He frowned now as the fortune-teller poured more desert sand into his palm and blew on it. She traced the tiny ridges which formed there.

"I see this man, *señor.* Riding a big horse. A man who laughs with the devil in his eyes . . . a handsome man. Younger than you . . . he is a close friend . . . of the same blood, perhaps . . . ah, yes . . . he is your

11

brother. He has been in trouble recently . . . with the law . . . and you sent for him. . . ."

Ben Corrin's palm trembled. Sweat beaded his upper lip . . . he eyed the old crone with narrowed gaze. "You see all this in my palm, old one?"

"In the lines of the sand, *señor*—the grains do not lie." She poured more sand into his palm and blew again. "I see—" Her lips sucked in sharply over worn gums. "The sand, *señor*. I am sorry—"

"What else do you see?" Ben demanded. Despite himself he was intensely interested now. He had assented to this old crone's reading while waiting in the cantina where he had just finished his dinner. He had time to kill in this small border town until Jeff arrived.

How had this old Mexican woman known that his brother was riding to meet him here? What else did she know?

"The sand, *señor*," the woman muttered. "It does not reveal itself. Perhaps another peso—?"

Corrin thrust an American half dollar into her fist. "What else, old one?"

She blew gently. She was humped over his palm, sharp bony shoulders jutting up, clothed in black, so that they looked like crow's wings.

She drew away, clutching her *rebozo* closer around her. She glanced toward the door.

"What did you see?"

"Another rider," she mumbled. Her voice was almost indistinct. "He does not look like a man who belongs here—he is dressed differently, *señor*. He will ride from

the south. Soon. And he will ride to the place where the long wire runs along the iron road—"

"The telegraph office?" Ben's voice held a strained wonder.

"Si, *señor*. He will come to this place and he will send a message. To someone far away. And you will speak to him, *señor*—I see it all here, in the grains of sand. You will speak to him and show him what you have in your pocket. And he—he—" She jerked her hand away and the movement spilled sand from Corrin's palm. She stood up, clutching the *rebozo* close around her.

"I cannot see the rest—the sand doesn't blow right. But, *senor* . . . do not bother with this man. Do not talk to him—"

"Why?" Corrin's tone was rough. Tension made the food he had just eaten lie heavy in his stomach. "Why shouldn't I see this man?"

She moved away. "I—I do not read more, *señor*. Only the warning. Do not interfere with this man—"

Ben Corrin stood up, but the old crone was already at the door. He sat back, conscious of the eyes of the round-faced proprietor on him. His hand trembled. He forced a smile to his lips.

What will Jeff say, he thought, when he tells him? Tough old Ranger getting all shook up because some hag blew sand on his palm and warned him!

But how did she know?

He got up and walked to the door of the cantina, his gaze narrowing to the glare of the sun on the sandy

street. He waited, leaning against the adobe wall. Unshaven, sandy-haired, blocky and of medium height, he didn't look much different from the others who walked the streets of this border town. Ansara was no more than a huddle of shacks in the desert. One was the depot and telegraph office, squatting by the iron rails that ran without a bend into the low, sage-stippled hills to the northeast—a place where the train stopped only on signal and where a freight car was detached perhaps once a month.

He put a Mexican cheroot between his teeth and lighted up and waited. He had wanted his brother here with him—he knew how close to the edge of lawlessness Jeff was standing.

A jury had found Jeff guilty of justifiable homicide. It turned him free, stripping him only of his Ranger badge. But it would be a long time before the bitterness within Jeff healed.

Ben sighed. If he could get Jeff reinstated as a Ranger—if he could get Jeff to work with him on this dangerous assignment he was on—it might ease the wildness in his younger brother.

Ben saw the rider now as he came up out of the arroyo just beyond the tracks and his thoughts steadied on the reason he had come to Ansara. The horseman wavered in the brutal midday heat, so Ben Corrin could not make out details. Still, the man did not have the appearance of the usual border rider.

Ben's teeth clenched hard on his cigar. *Briscole!* He

had not expected this man to show so soon—had not expected him until tomorrow!

The rider was headed straight for the telegraph office. The words of the old fortune-teller echoed in Bens ears.

Do not interfere with this man!

He couldn't let this man go. But there was cold sweat on Ranger Corrin's brow as he pushed away from the cantina wall. It was five hundred long yards to the small depot.

He glanced once toward the north where a brown ribbon of trail showed among the near hills. Jeff would be riding that trail. But the road was empty as far as he could see.

The rider had dismounted and was walking to the telegraph window when Ben mounted the steps to the loading platform. The newcomer was taller than Ben by a head—a heavy-shouldered, handsome man with a clipped military mustache and bright blue eyes. He was at the window, thrusting a sheaf of handwritten papers through the window.

"I'm Roger Briscole," the man said. "Special correspondent for the *New York World*. I want this sent collect to Editor David Hall—"

He turned as Ben approached. Briscole was wearing a white shirt, stained from desert riding, and sand-colored whipcord britches. His black string tie was unknotted, the ends trailing down his shirt.

Ben said coldly, "Mr. Briscole?"

The man nodded, frowning.

"Come with me, please."

Briscole's eyes narrowed. "Just a moment, sir. Who are you?"

Ben Corrin slipped his left hand out of his coat pocket. He held his badge briefly to the other's gaze.

"I want a word with you," he said quietly.

Briscole nodded. His face was dark burned by the sun. He showed only a polite interest. "Why, of course, Ranger."

He walked along the length of the platform with Corrin. "I'd like to lead my horse to wherever you're going?"

Corrin shrugged. He didn't see a gun on Briscole, and if this man was who he claimed to be, he wouldn't be carrying one. But Ben was certain that he was not the *New York World* correspondent.

He waited on the edge of the platform while the Ranger went down the steps and picked up the reins of his cayuse. The sun beat down over the iron rails, sending heat waves shimmering. There was a small movement against the base of a mesquite clinging to the edge of the arroyo from which the rider had come. But Ben Corrin didn't see it.

Briscole hesitated on the platform, smiling down at Ben. "Hot," he said. He reached up and pushed his cream-colored Stetson back on his head.

The rifle bullet from the arroyo hit Ben high in the side, jerking him around. He made a grab for his holster gun but the second shot knocked his right leg from

under him. He fell heavily and rolled against the platform and then lay still.

Briscole swung into the saddle of his waiting horse. He was dipping down into the arroyo, three hundred yards away, when Bob Callings, station agent and telegrapher, came running out to the platform.

Ben Corrin was still breathing when the station agent jumped down beside him. Ben was trying to get up, spitting blood. His voice was a half sob of pain and rage: "Get me inside, Bob. I—I need a pencil and paper . . . it's important. . . ."

A half dozen Mexican townsmen straggled up, their movements cautious. It was generally unhealthy to investigate too soon the source of gunshots.

Callings turned to them. "Give me a hand with him, Juan. Lopez, run over to Ladetto's house. Fetch that horse doctor pronto, if he ain't too drunk to walk!"

They carried Ben into the station, laid him out on a bench. He fought off their attempts to make him lie down. "Pencil . . . paper . . ." he snarled. "Got to write something down . . . something for my brother . . . Jeff . . ."

Callings shrugged. He and Juan helped Ben to the nearby desk, sat him down. Callings brought out some paper and a pencil.

They stood by while Ben Corrin wrote. The Ranger paused, his eyes clouding, fighting the pain tearing inside him.

He finished, folded the paper. He beckoned to the lanky station agent. "Rider will be coming to town

soon . . . 'fore sundown. My brother—Jeff. See that he gets this . . ."

Callings nodded. "Better rest now." He and Juan brought Ben back to the bench, laid him down.

Ben muttered: "It's important . . . tell Jeff . . ."

Callings walked to the door, looked out. What was keeping Ladetto?

Across the barren flats, in the distance, he could see the faint dust banner of two riders heading for the low, desolate hills of Chihuahua. He shook his head in bewilderment.

He walked back to his desk and picked up the message Roger Briscole had given him. It was an eyewitness account, a special report to the *New York World* concerning the activities of the Mexican revolutionary band that called itself *The Amigos*.

Callings read the story. *Amigos, hell!* he thought sourly. Border killers would be the better name for them. But the *World*'s special correspondent was calling them Mexico's hope for the future.

He turned as a short, swarthy man in rumpled clothes came inside, trailed by several townsmen. Ladetto was primarily a veterinarian, but he treated human ailments as well. He walked over to Ben, frowned, put the back of his hand against Ben's open mouth. Then he turned and looked sharply at the station agent.

"*Señor,*" he growled. "This man is dead."

III

JEFF CORRIN came to the town of Ansara at sundown. Bob Callings was waiting for him on the depot platform; he had been waiting for Ben's brother to show up a long time now.

He walked to the middle of the sandy road to meet him.

"Jeff Corrin?"

Jeff edged his horse aside and studied the lanky, shirt-sleeved man with the green eyeshade. Then his glance flicked to the small group of men waiting just beyond, in front of the Cantina.

He knew then that something had happened to Ben.

"I'm Jeff Corrin," he acknowledged.

"Man inside my office said to wait for you," Callings explained. His voice was respectful. He had seen a lot of men in his time here; most of the riders who came through Ansara were a rough, dangerous breed. This man was like them, and yet not like them—there was a hardness in Jeff that went deeper than mere bone and muscle.

He's dead," Callings went on. "But he said to give a rider name of Jeff Corrin this message . . ."

Jeff dismounted and took the folded paper from the station agent and read it. He read it slowly, his face

revealing nothing to the watching men. Then he folded the paper, tucked it into his pocket.

"I'll take a look at him."

They went inside and Jeff stood by the blanket-covered figure for a moment before reaching down, lifting a corner from Ben's face. He glanced at the still features, then dropped the blanket. He slowly made himself a cigarette.

He and Ben had always gotten along fine although ten years had separated them . . . he had grown to manhood looking up to his older, more amiable brother.

Go ahead, get married, kid, Ben had told him once. *It'll make a man out of you!*

Ben had laughed as he said it, but he had been serious. He was married himself, and the father of three children, all of whom adored Uncle Jeff.

Then Jeff had taken up with a girl . . . a farm girl name of Ellen Larkin. They had planned a wedding . . . it had been a Saturday night . . . and that was the last time Jeff saw Ellen alive.

Two men had ridden by the farm, killed Ellen's father and mother, raped Ellen and left her to die. They had done all this for forty dollars—all the money the Larkins had in the house.

Jeff had just been recruited as a Texas Ranger. He trailed the two men. And killed them. As an officer of the law his job had been to bring them back for trial . . . it was not within his authority to act as judge and executioner.

The jury had been understanding. Captain Hawkins

at Ranger Headquarters had been less forgiving. A martinet, he did not want a man on his staff who forgot he was wearing a badge.

It had not mattered much to Jeff then, turning in his badge—it did not matter much now. But Ben had wanted him back . . . and now, looking down at his dead brother, he felt he owed Ben that much.

He went to the message counter and wrote out two messages. One was to Ben's wife, Lottie. There was not much he could say to his sister-in-law . . . his words of sympathy had a hollow sound.

He sent the other message to Captain Hawkins, Texas Ranger Headquarters.

Then he questioned Callings as to what happened.

"Man named Roger Briscole came to the window to send a wire to New York," Callings told him. "Said he was from the *New York World,* a special correspondent. Then your brother came in . . . they walked out together. I was getting ready to send the story to New York when I heard the shots outside."

"You didn't see who killed Ben?"

Callings shook his head. "He rode into town alone, that Briscole fellow. But when I came out there were two riders heading south. They were quite a ways off, but one of them was Roger Briscole."

Jeff was still a moment, his eyes hard, thoughtful. "That newspaperman's story—you still have it?"

The station agent nodded. "Some tripe about that band of Mexican revolutionaries, the *Amigos.* Sounds like this Briscole fellow is riding with them. He sure

21

paints a pretty picture of those damn killers, if you ask me . . ."

Jeff read the story. Callings was right. If anyone believed this story, then *Vincente Avilla,* the rebel leader, was a kind, patient man anxious only to lead his peasant people to the promised land. A great man of noble intention, centering on liberty and peace . . .

He tossed the story back on Callings' desk and went out.

He was in the Cantina, having a drink, when Captain Hawkins' answer was delivered to him.

The message was blunt.

"Sorry about Ben. We will handle burial. Can't comply with your request for reinstatement as Texas Ranger. My advice—don't go into Mexico. Stay out of trouble.

Jeff crumpled the telegram in his fist. He brought out Ben's scribbled note, read it carefully.

He left Ansara before the moon was up . . . he rode south, into Mexico.

IV

THE DESERT SUN cracked the dry and broken land and the hills were hot and stony. The air clung to Jeff, encasing him as in an oven . . . he paused and eased

his saddle and rifle down and spat a thin dry spittle
that left no impression on the burning ground.

A horned toad looked up from the shady protection
of a small rock. Beady eyes stared briefly at him, then
the lids hooded over . . . he crouched motionless, a
relic of life from the past.

"You said it," Jeff muttered. He straightened up and
looked toward the hills, squinting against the glare
of the sun. They seemed utterly barren, absolutely lifeless.

There was no trail of any kind leading this way . . .
yet Jeff knew there was a spring and a small stone
shack just beyond the butte with the massive overhang
of rock and the wind-tortured juniper sprouting from
the top.

His brother had learned this much about the *Amigos*.

Jeff glanced back the way he had come. He had
sought the hard places, the rocky stretches where his
boots left no visible prints—he did not want to be
backtracked.

He pushed his hat back on his head and wiped his
face with the back of his sleeve as he looked around.
He made his glance casual, like a man who's undecided which way to go. He unslung his canteen from
his shoulder, shook it. It was almost empty—this part of
his deception would be real, he thought, and finished
it off. The water tasted dry—it slid down his throat
without wetting it . . . it was gone and not even the
memory of it was wet.

Jeff picked up his saddle and started to walk toward

the butte. He knew he was being watched—he felt the skin at the back of his neck prickle and his eyes hooded. He had the sudden, sick feeling that his life was hanging on the pressure of a trigger finger—it was being weighed in the watcher's mind, and he was powerless to influence it or affect it.

He kept walking, however, like a man who is lost and completely unaware of anyone within fifty miles. He rested several times—and this was no act, the tiredness with which he sank down.

A half hour later he passed through a gash in the long butte and followed a desert runoff whose dry bed was thick with rocks washed down from above. Spiny shrubs clung to the reddish banks. He followed this until he came to the crest and looked down into a small pocket amidst the burning hills.

To Jeff it was like looking into a cool, clean land. Even the air felt cool. There was green down there, feathery cottonwoods, a stone hut and stone corrals. A dozen horses were bunched together at the north end of the corral, seeking the shade of the pepper tree arching like a green umbrella over them. He saw a bird flit among the green and it was the first sign of winged life Jeff had seen since morning.

He heaved his saddle across his shoulder again and started at a faster pace down the slope, heading for the pool of water he glimpsed between the trees. Reaching it, he sank down and ducked his head into the cool water—he raised his head, then, and sloshed some of the water down his back.

Then he drank, cupping the water in his hands.

He heard the low *whoosh,* an animal sound low and savage in a shaggy throat, and he came up and around just in time to meet the spring of a big, wolflike dog.

The dog came for his throat in a silent, deadly leap. Jeff swerved and cuffed it on the side of its head, a panther-quick blow that slammed the animal down hard on the spongy ground. The dog scrambled up and leaped again and this time Jeff caught it under the shaggy throat and whirled it around, sending the seventy pound animal into the pool.

He waited, his hand on his Colt butt, watching the dog start to paddle for the shore.

"First time any man ever handled Wolf like that," a voice said. It was a nasal voice—it had the quality of disuse in it.

Jeff turned. A gaunt, shabby man in faded bib Levis and dirty underwear faced him. He carried a rifle in his right hand, held carelessly . . . he was a sun-dried, sinewy slab of a man as tall as Jeff. His face was like the land, too, brown and eroded and stubbled with a peppery beard—his mouth was slack and tobacco juice stained his chin.

Jeff glanced at the hut. "Your place?"

The gaunt man nodded.

"I want to buy a horse." Jeff kept the corner of his gaze on the shaggy dog, who had emerged from the pool and was shaking himself dry.

"Ain't got none," the gaunt man said. He didn't move from where he was standing.

25

But the dog crouched now, began to move toward Jeff on his belly.

"Your dog?" Jeff's voice was hard.

"Yup."

"Tell him to behave, then. Or you'll lose him."

The gaunt man considered this. Then he nodded. "Wolf!" he called sharply. "Git back to the house. Git!"

Wolf growled rebelliously. But he got up off his belly, backed off, then turned and went loping toward the hut.

"I counted a dozen cayuses from the top of the hill," Jeff said.

"Ain't got none," the gaunt man repeated calmly. "None for sale."

Jeff's eyes narrowed. "I'll give you a hundred dollars for the worst one in your corral—"

The gaunt man's eyes glittered with sudden greed. "Might consider it. How much you got?"

"The hundred I offered you, no more!"

The gaunt man cackled. "Hear him, Jack? He's talkin' tough!"

A shorter man came into Jeff's sight now, pausing by one of the cottonwoods. He was younger and wiry and a good deal cleaner—he had recently bought a gray hat and new boots. The gun in his right hand was new, too—or the muzzle had been recently blued.

"You want a horse?" he asked. "Why?"

Jeff eyed them both—he saw that he was whipsawed between them—the gaunt man with the rifle and the younger one holding a Colt.

"Ran into an Apache war party," he said. "They killed my horse."

Jack's eyes narrowed. "Medano's tribe has been shut up in Fort Gower for two weeks, pending an investigation. Ain't been an Apache off the reservation within ninety miles."

Jeff shrugged. "Would a posse suit you better? A bad fall—a broken leg?"

Jack sneered. "It might."

He made a motion with his gun. "Fancy looking hardware for a down-at-the-heels drifter. Take your gun out slow and toss it to me."

Jeff hesitated.

The gaunt man said: "The kid ain't foolin', mister."

Jeff shrugged. He started to reach for his Colt—then his hand blurred and there was a puff of smoke at his hip and Jack's hand jerked as his gun spun out of it.

Jeff swung sharply, his muzzle targeting the gaunt man. The older man dropped his rifle.

Jack stood still, his lips curled, half in pain, half in unbelief. His hand bled from the bullet gash across his knuckles.

Jeff said coldly: "I'm still willing to pay a hundred dollars in gold for a horse. But now I'll want the best you have in that corral—I'll pick him out myself!"

There was a long moment of silence. Then a voice from beyond Jeff said: "Let him have a horse, Phineas."

There were a half dozen riders just beyond the trees behind Jeff, waiting there as though they had

formed out of thin air. Five of them were men. The sixth was a girl.

She was young, strikingly beautiful, blonde—a startling contrast to the men she rode with. She studied Jeff with little interest . . . there was a cold arrogance in this girl that put her above her surroundings.

The man beside her was lean and hawklike, about forty . . . and with a dusty, frayed brush jacket crossed by cartridge bandoliers. He had bright black, restless eyes in which burned a bitter cynical fire. He wore an anthill hat, thus deliberately setting himself apart from the four men with him . . . he was Mexican and they were not, and yet—without making a move or saying anything—he dominated them, overshadowed them.

He leaned forward over his saddle horn now, a faint smile on his face as he looked at Jeff. His hands were small, brown, quick—they gave the impression of quickness even in repose.

"Not many men find their way to Escondido Valley, *amigo*. What brings you here?"

Jeff still had his Colt in his fist, but he knew he'd be dead if he made a wrong move with it. Very slowly he eased it back into his holster.

"You have not answered," the Mexican said. There was a threat in the softness of his voice and Jeff knew without ever having met the man that he was looking at Vincente Avilla. He was not what Jeff had expected. This was no uneducated peon with a drive for power, using the time-worn cliché of freedom for the common people of Mexico as a leverage to political power.

Nor were the men with him Mexican. They were Americans—gun-handy adventurers whose only allegiance was to gold, Mexican or otherwise.

"I lost my horse back on the desert," he said. "I just started walking—"

"And stumbled on this little valley, my friend?"

"Yeah—lucky for me," Jeff nodded. "Spotted those horses in the corral—" He shrugged. "I'm headed for Vera Cruz."

Vincente Avilla leaned forward over his saddle horn. "Vera Cruz, my friend, is a long way off. And these are troubled times in Mexico."

"So I've heard."

Avilla glanced at Phineas and Jack; he seemed to be judging something in his mind.

"I am Vincente Avilla," he said to Jeff. "You have heard of me?"

Jeff nodded. "Good and bad. You are the boss of the *Amigos*."

Vincente eyed him. "Their leader," he said coldly. He turned to the man next to him. The man's left ear was missing, only a misshapen lump of flesh where it had been. He had a steel wire body under dusty clothes, and a young but incredibly ugly face.

"This is Silent Gordon, my *segundo*." There was a faint mockery in Avilla's voice now. "Silent is a lover of freedom—a deadly enemy of Mexico's oppressors." He pointed to the others with him: Nogales Smith, a runty, balding man with blue eyes in a round, almost cherubic face. He had a limp cigarette in his mouth. Nat

Hines was a stocky man who looked like an unsuccessful rancher. Cob Eaton was taller, with emotionless features. All of them were heavily armed, deadly.

"And—my niece, Maria," Vincente concluded. He looked at Jeff, smiling. "And you—my friend—who are you?"

"Pete," Jeff said . . . "Pete Galahad."

The girl stirred and interest quickened in her eyes. Vincente scowled. "Galahad?"

"You want a name," Jeff said. "Galahad's as good as any."

Vincente studied him, his eyes narrowing. "You mock me, *señor?*"

Jeff licked his lips. He had to play the role of a tough, drifting gunhand . . . but he knew he could push this man only so far.

"I'm trying to get to Vera Cruz," he temporized. "It doesn't matter who I really am."

Vincente said nothing for a moment, then nodded, relaxing slightly. "No, it doesn't," he said softly. He turned slightly and raised his right hand shoulder high and the guns of the four men riding with him were suddenly drawn, trained on Jeff.

"I am sorry," he said to Jeff . . . "but I cannot let you go on. . . ."

"Wait!" Maria moved her cayuse closer to the Mexican leader. "Let father talk to him."

Avilla looked at his niece.

"You know his rules," the girl repeated firmly. "All strangers are brought to him first. He decides."

Vincente sighed.

"Take his gun, Phineas."

Phineas edged toward Jeff, paused as Jeff turned slightly to face him. He had seen what a gun in Jeff's hand could do.

Jeff looked at the Mexican boss of the *Amigos*. "Just so you get one thing straight, Avilla. That girl just saved your life."

He tossed his gun to Phineas who caught it, startled. Vincente smiled. "I think George will be glad to see you," he said.

He swung around to Jack.

"Get him a horse. We're riding."

V

THE *Paseo Grande* ranch spread out along the small and forgotten river, shaded by trees planted more than a hundred years before Father Kingo and his followers. The ruins of an old Spanish presidio looked down from the rocky cliffs beyond, and around a bend in the river was an ancient mission church, its bell tower gone, its walls crumbling.

Until a month ago Father Ortegano rode a mule from Durango to say mass at the church, but now, with trouble flaring all along the northern border, it had become too hazardous to make the journey.

Virtually isolated, big and cattle rich, the ranch had become an armed camp.

The tall man standing at the window of his room was reminded of this as the Mexican sentry paced past his line of vision.

Roger Briscole watched him for a moment, then lifted his gaze past the run of cooling trees to the hot, sterile hills that marked the borders of the savage country beyond the ranch.

Way off in the distance, coming down the old presidio trail, Roger saw riders . . . he turned and picked up a pair of field glasses from a table (a small luxury allowed him) and turned back to the window.

The glasses brought the indistinct figures into focus ; . . he could make out Avilla and Maria. He knew the others . . . but the man riding between Avilla and Maria was a stranger. Briscole, though, felt only a sadness for Avilla as he thought: *Another gun for a revolution that would never take place.* . . .

He turned as he heard someone open the door and come into the room behind him. It was a large, airy room in which he was being held prisoner . . . beamed with rough-hewn timbers, the thick adobe walls whitewashed a creamy coolness. Hand-woven Indian tapestries added color to the otherwise meagerly furnished chamber . . . there was a bed, again of heavy timbers, a chest, a mirror and a long trestle table.

The man who came into the room was as tall as Briscole, but better looking and more sure of himself . . . he had passed himself off as the newspaperman

at Ansara, but his real name was Cass Borman and he managed this ranch for George Taine.

He strode up to Briscole, a big man in immaculate whipcord trousers and white shirt, the black string tie ends loose, giving him an air of relaxed competence. A good-looking man in his middle thirties (a few years older than Briscole) he wore a clipped military mustache that somehow enhanced his appearance as a manager of American holdings in a foreign land.

"Missed you at dinner," Cass said, smiling.

The newspaperman shrugged. "I'm not very hungry—"

"You look a little poorly," Cass said. He took the field glasses from Briscole. "You need a change . . . a chance to get out of this room." He started to lift the glasses to his eyes.

"Maybe I can arrange a boar hunt. Ever hunt one of these devils? The Mexicans call them *javellinos—?*"

He was studying the far-off riders through the glasses. But he caught Briscole's headshake from the corner of his eye.

Cass lowered the glasses; he put a hand on Roger's shoulder.

"What do you want, Roger?" His tone was friendly. "George said to make sure you were comfortable. You haven't wanted for anything, have you?"

Roger looked him in the eye. "Let me ride out of here, Cass!"

Cass kept his smile, but his eyes were ice blue and ruthlessly direct.

"You know that's impossible."

Roger turned away from him.

Cass studied him for a moment. "It's your own fault, you know. If you'd change your mind about the revolution—"

Briscole's tone was bitter: "What revolution?"

"Avilla's revolution," Cass answered smoothly. "The hope of the poor starving peasants of this country—"

He broke off as Avilla and his group came into sight again down the long, tree-shaded road to the ranch-yard. He placed the field glasses down on the table.

Roger said bitterly: "The peasants will take care of themselves, eventually. I'm sorry for Vincente Avilla."

Cass looked at him, his eyes cold. "Don't be. Vince is getting what he wants out of this."

He turned and left the room. Roger remained by the window, staring out at the hot, desolate hills. . . .

Coming down the tree-shaded road Jeff Corrin could see Texas cattle in the corrals . . . a mixture of long-horn and Hereford and some Brahmas. He also saw armed men all along the way and the feeling came to him that this big ranch was like a fort, self-sufficient and contained and impervious to the troubles around it.

Cass Borman was waiting on the wide and awning-shaded veranda as they rode into the yard. He had an Army holster and Colt belted at his side . . . he came to the head of the steps and smiled at Maria and there was genuine feeling in his eyes.

"Glad to see you back, Maria."

The girl swung down from the saddle like a man . . . she had a man's way of riding and it was obvious she had spent much time on a horse. And yet she retained a soft and feminine aura . . . one never mistook her for anything but a woman.

She looked up at Cass, not sharing his feelings.

"Where's father?"

"Left for Durango . . . right after you left."

Maria was disappointed.

Avilla had dismounted . . . a Mexican ranch hand was coming up to take care of the horse.

"On business again, Cass?" Avilla's voice was casual.

Cass nodded. He watched the Mexican leader come up the veranda steps and pick up the dipper by the big *olla*. He swung his gaze back to Jeff who alone remained in saddle.

"Where'd you pick him up, Vince?"

Avilla glanced at Jeff. "Escondido Valley. He was looking for a horse . . ."

Jeff put in, evenly: "All I wanted was a horse, Mister. I won't bother anybody. I'm headed for Vera Cruz."

Cass looked at Avilla. "Why didn't you give him a horse and let him go?"

Vincente studied Borman, his eyes lidded. Then: "I don't believe him."

Cass smiled. "Then I guess there's only one thing to do. Shoot him!"

Maria was shocked. *"Cass!"*

Avilla shrugged. He dipped into the clay water jug

35

and drank, like an Apache, just enough to ease the dryness in his mouth.

Cass was looking at the girl, his eyebrows arched slightly. "For all we know he might be a murderer—"

"Even a murderer gets a trial," Maria said sharply. "You can't just—"

"These are troubled times in Mexico," Cass cut in smoothly. "We can't always observe the niceties of the law." He looked at Avilla.

"What do you say, Vince?"

Vince eyed Jeff casually. "He's fast with a gun. That could be good—or bad. Depends on what side he's on—"

Maria cut in: "You promised to let father decide—"

Avilla looked at Cass who shrugged. He motioned to Jeff.

"Get down."

Jeff swung out of saddle. His life was hanging on the whim of these two men, both casual as to their decision. . . .

The ranch hand had gathered up the reins of the horses and was starting to lead them toward the corral . . . Jeff started to move aside, then suddenly whirled, lifted a rifle from one of the saddles, whirled and cocked it in one quick motion.

He leveled the muzzle at Cass.

No one moved.

Surprise and chagrin held the men who had ridden with Jeff and Avilla. Vincente came to stand beside Cass.

He murmured: "See what I mean, Cass?"

Jeff said grimly: "I'll trade you, mister." He was speaking to Cass. "Your life—for a horse."

Cass shook his head.

"You've got five seconds!" Jeff said. He meant it.

Nogales Smith began to ease away, his hand inching toward his gun. Avilla made a slight head motion—Nogales stopped.

Maria said sharply: "Put that gun away, Galahad!"

She walked directly in front of the muzzle, put her hand on it, pushed it aside. "I'll make the trade—"

Jeff tried to push her away . . . Silent Gordon came up behind his head.

Jeff fell against the girl and went down, unconscious. She picked up the rifle as Silent Gordon started to point the muzzle of his gun at the back of Jeff's head.

She looked at Cass. "I saved your life. I want his . . ."

Cass shrugged. "What about it, Vince?"

Vince was looking at Jeff sprawled in front of the steps.

"Maybe we're making a mistake," he said. "But I always like a man who puts up a fight." He turned to Gordon. "Take him over to the bunkhouse. When he's ready to ride, if Mr. Taine isn't back, give him a horse and ride with him as far as the old presidio . . ."

He looked at Maria, his voice softening. "That all right with you, Maria?"

She nodded.

Cass waved to the door. "Come on in. Must be close to a hundred out in that sun . . ."

As Avilla and Maria mounted the steps, Cass glanced toward the men hauling Jeff toward the bunkhouse.

"Galahad?"

He smiled, but his eyes were cold and he would always remember that for a few seconds he had been at the mercy of that unconscious stranger.

VI

Nogales Smith squatted by the bunk, his back up against a post and watched as Jeff frowned slightly and reached out with his right hand as if groping for something. He watched with bright-eyed interest, saying nothing until Jeff opened his eyes and turned his head toward him.

The bunkhouse was long and narrow. It had been built barracks-style, with doors at both ends open to catch the breeze. Inside the thick adobe walls it was at least twenty degrees cooler.

Except for Nogales and Jeff the bunkhouse was empty. The runty outlaw said casually: "I was about to give up on you, Galahad."

He held up three fingers. "How many?" He held them close to Jeff's face.

Jeff's pain-filled eyes focused slowly . . . he shifted his gaze to Nogales, who repeated the question.

"Three," he muttered and pushed himself up into a

sitting position and ran his fingers slowly down the bruise on the back of his head.

Nogales grinned. His voice was casual. "Guess you're all right." He straightened. "Feel like eating?"

Jeff ran his tongue across his lips. "Thirsty."

Nogales walked to the big clay jar standing by the door . . . there was a cover over the mouth to keep out insects. He brought Jeff a dipper of lukewarm water.

Jeff drank it all. Nogales hunkered down again, watching. Jeff touched the lump on his head again. He looked at the gunslinger. "Who?" His voice was hard, angry.

"You're lucky to be alive," Nogales said. He walked to the door, looked out toward the gallery. Dishes clattering and men's rough voices drifted back. He turned to Jeff. "You sure you're not hungry?"

Jeff swung his legs over the bunk and stood up and unconsciously dropped his hand to his empty holster. He looked at Nogales, his eyes questioning.

"You'll get your Colt later." Nogales gestured to the gallery. "You better come along, Galahad. They feed well here."

Jeff joined the small man at the door. There was a dull pain at the back of his head and his legs were weak, as though he had been a long time in a sick bed.

He leaned against the door jamb and looked across the big ranchyard . . . the galley was a square building closer to the creek.

He nodded. "I'll give it a try."

They walked the hundred yards to the galley. The *Paseo Grande* ranch, he learned later, had a caste sys-

tem . . . its hired hands ate in shifts, the Americans first, the Mexican ranch hands last. Perhaps for compensation, but mostly because of tradition, the Mexicans had a longer siesta period.

Besides Silent Gordon, Cob Eaton and Nat Hines, whom Jeff had met, there were at least a dozen other American gunhands. They gave Jeff a cursory glance and went on eating.

Jeff eased onto a long bench beside Nogales. Gordon sat across from him. The ugly *segundo* eyed him briefly.

"You feel up to riding?"

Jeff looked at him.

Gordon said: "Boss said you could go." He waved to the platters of food. "Go ahead and eat." His grin had a cold wickedness rather than warmth. "Be a long time between meals after you leave here."

Nogales was heaping his plate with steak, potatoes, beans, tortillas and everything else he saw on the table. He was, Jeff observed without interest, a small man with a big appetite.

Jeff ate very little. He drank a lot of water.

Gordon finished and rolled himself a cigarette. He watched Jeff for a minute, then: "You through?"

Jeff nodded.

Gordon stood up. "Let's go."

He motioned to Nat Hines who pushed away from the table and joined Silent, the others watching curiously. The three of them went out to the corral.

Jeff said: "What changed the boss' mind?"

"Mr. Borman?" Silent shrugged. "Reckon it was Miss

Taine." He paused at the corral bars. "She's the only one around here can get what she wants from Borman. And her uncle Vince," he added casually.

Jeff frowned. "Miss Taine?" The name had a familiar ring, tantalizing him. Yet he knew he had never seen this girl before.

Gordon nodded. "George Taine's daughter. Taine owns this place—but Cass Borman runs it."

He waved toward a half dozen horses huddled in the shade of an old pepper tree inside the corral.

"Take your pick."

Jeff moved close to the corral bars, studying the grouped animals . . . the name of George Taine now clicked into place. A big man in Texas—friend of the governor, chummy with a state senator, owner of a big ranch just north of Eagle Pass, the Triangle T.

Jeff knew George Taine, having met the rancher at Ranger headquarters once or twice—and George Taine would remember him.

Maria and Vincente Avilla came out of the ranch house to watch. The *Amigos'* boss remained on the veranda, being joined by Borman a few moments later—but Maria joined Jeff at the corral.

Her smile was friendly enough. "How do you feel now, Galahad?"

Jeff shrugged. "Well enough."

"I saved your life," she said casually. "Aren't you going to thank me?"

He looked at her for a long moment and she began

to flush. Gordon's eyes narrowed and his hand slid down toward his gun.

"Thanks," Jeff said dryly.

Her voice was cold now. "Gordon and Hines will ride with you until you're clear of the ranch. Vera Cruz is southeast. You'll have to find your own way."

Jeff turned to the ugly *segundo,* extending his right hand. "I'll need my gun. I'm not looking for trouble, but with things the way they are in Mexico it might be hard to avoid it."

Gordon glanced at Maria who nodded. He turned to Nat Hines, lounging against the corral bars.

"Get his gun."

Nat Hines went into the bunkhouse.

Maria said: "You don't like Mexico, do you?" There was a faint resentment in her voice.

Jeff was watching the two men on the veranda . . . his attention drifted to a window of the sprawling ranch house, half shrouded by shrubbery . . . he glimpsed a man standing by the window, inside the house, looking out. . . .

Roger Briscole?

Maria's sharp voice intruded into his speculation: "Do you?"

He put his gaze on her, his voice level: "I didn't come here for my health, Miss Taine."

She nodded. "Father is due back any time." She turned to Gordon. "Maybe we should wait—"

Nat Hines appeared, holding Jeff's sixgun. He handed it to Gordon.

The last thing Jeff wanted was to meet her father. He said harshly: "I don't like being the mouse in a cat-and-mouse game. Am I leaving—or staying?"

Maria looked at Gordon. "Give him his gun."

Gordon handed the weapon to Jeff. "It's empty," he said. "You've got shells in your cartridge belt. Don't reload until you're on your way to Vera Cruz."

Jeff slipped the gun into his holster.

"I'll take the roan," he said, waving toward the horses in the corral. "The one with the left front stocking."

Gordon signaled to a Mexican wrangler hunkered down, smoking, in the thin shadow cast by the barn. The man shuffled over. He was in his fifties—a seamed, leathery-faced man with a slight limp. He looked at Maria for orders, ignoring Gordon and Hines. She told him in Spanish what she wanted; he nodded and went into the barn for a rope.

Maria turned to Jeff. "If you weren't so quarrelsome," she said lightly, "my uncle could use you. But he doesn't trust you—"

"Revolution isn't my line," Jeff cut in.

"What is?" Gordon asked. He looked amused. "Bank holdups? Stagecoaches? Or just plain murder?"

Jeff looked at them, reacting to the amused lightness of their conversation. They were smug; he was just a drifter they were being momentarily kind to.

He turned away toward the corral gate.

Silent reached out, yanked him around.

"When you're asked a question around here, answer it!"

Jeff knocked his hand away. "Go to hell!"

Silent instinctively went for his gun. Jeff drove his fist into Silent's ugly face, knocking him back against the corral bars . . . he stepped in quickly, before the *segundo* could recover and sank his fist into the gunman's stomach.

Silent doubled up and dropped his gun and Jeff stepped on it, then froze as he heard a gun cock behind him.

"Nat, no!"

He turned slowly to Maria's voice . . . she was standing between him and Hines, who had a gun leveled in his hand.

Nat Hines slowly put his gun away.

Maria turned to Jeff, her face blazing. "Next time I'll let them shoot you!"

Jeff said levelly: "I don't take to being shoved around."

Maria shook her head. "With that temper I really don't know how you've managed to live this long."

She turned to Gordon, who was braced against the corral bars, breathing with difficulty—the gunman lifted his finger tips to probe at his cut lip.

"Go lie down in the bunkhouse," Maria suggested. "I'll get someone else to ride with him."

Silent pushed her away . . . he took an unsteady step toward Jeff, his eyes hating. . . .

Avilla's voice stopped him. "Gordon!"

The *Amigos'* boss and Cass Borman were coming toward them. Avilla pointed toward the bunkhouse. "Do as Maria says."

Gordon looked at Jeff. "Some day I'm going to kill you!"

He picked up his gun, jammed it into his holster and walked slowly to the bunkhouse.

Avilla and Borman paused beside Maria. Avilla's gaze was curious, studying Jeff.

Borman's smile was more a sneer. "You're the most untactful man I've ever met. You're just begging to be killed."

Jeff said grimly: "I didn't ask to come here."

Maria intervened, her face flaming. "No, you didn't. And the sooner you leave, the better!"

The Mexican wrangler was at the corral gate with Jeff's roan, saddled and ready.

As Jeff started to mount, Maria said: "Just a moment." As Jeff turned: "He'll cost you one hundred dollars."

Jeff shook his head.

Avilla moved up beside his niece, smiling a little. Borman's eyes were cold. "We're not giving you that horse, Galahad."

Maria said, "You told us at Escondido Valley that you would pay that much for a horse—"

"That was then," Jeff interrupted grimly. He touched the bump at the back of his head. "Way I figger it now, you owe me this horse."

Maria stared at him, shocked at the unmitigated gall of the man. Then she exploded: "Why, you . . . you . . ." she spluttered, at a loss for the proper ladylike words.

Avilla made a quick gesture to the saddled roan. "Go on," he said harshly to Jeff. "Get out of here!"

Jeff swung aboard.

"Just keep riding," the boss of the *Amigos* added grimly. He waved a hand southward.

Jeff reached down for the canteen hanging from his saddle. It felt empty. He shook it to make sure.

Avilla grinned coldly. "*Señor,* for a man such as you, what is water? There are springs out there in the desert . . . somewhere. . . ."

Jeff eyed him. Cass Borman was smiling . . . Maria was too angry to care.

"The desert, *señor,*" Avilla said harshly. "Or a bullet. It is your choice."

Jeff studied the three of them for a long hard moment, then he started to swing away.

Borman said: "Ride with him, Nat. See that he gets a good long start for Vera Cruz."

As Hines started for his horse the Mexican wrangler suddenly pointed toward the tree-shaded road.

"El patrone!"

Jeff turned, a chill sluicing through him.

Three riders flanked the fringe-topped buggy that rolled at the head of four canvas-covered wagons. The driver of the buggy was a Mexican. The big fleshy man on the seat beside him, in wilted white shirt and rumpled town clothes was George Taine.

They swept into the yard, the American armed guard grim-faced, dust-covered. George Taine turned and motioned the wagons to a stop. Then, glancing toward the

small group by the corral, he said something to his driver. The buggy swung toward them.

Jeff sat rigid in his saddle.

The buggy pulled up a few feet away. Taine glanced at Jeff, then put his attention on Avilla, Cass and his daughter.

"I've got the guns," he said to Borman. Then, to Avilla. "There's a military contingent coming up out of Mexico City, headed by General Franco. They'll be in Durango in three days . . ."

Avilla nodded, a brightness in his eyes.

Taine started to step down from his buggy. He paused, glanced at Jeff, then looked startled, recognizing the ex-Texas Ranger.

Borman was watching him; he said sharply: "You know this man, George?"

Taine looked steadily into Jeff's cold eyes . . . after a long moment he took a breath, shook his head. "No. For a moment I thought I did—"

Borman pressed him. "You sure?"

Taine swung his attention to Cass; he was a man of hard temper. "Of course. Who is he?"

Avilla answered: "Found him at Escondido Valley. Fast with a gun." He smiled faintly. "A man with a mean temper—he said he was looking for a horse—"

"So *he* said," Borman cut in harshly. "I don't believe him, George. Neither does Vince."

Taine pinned his cold glance on Jeff. "Get down!"

Jeff hesitated, then dismounted.

"What do you call yourself?"

"Pete Galahad."

A flicker of amusement went through Taine's eyes. "Give me thirty minutes to get washed and rested. Then come to the ranch house. I want to talk to you."

He started for the house.

Borman said: "He's trouble, George."

Taine looked at him. "We ran into a bit of trouble picking up those guns. We lost Nick. We can use a replacement."

He took his daughter's arm. They went into the ranch house, and Jeff, unnoticed, let out a long, slow breath of puzzled relief.

VII

BORMAN WAITED until Taine and Maria had gone into the ranch house. He slapped his palm gently against his holster, his only outward sign of anger . . . his eyes studied Jeff, narrowed and suspicious.

"You'd be better off heading for Vera Cruz," he suggested. "I'll tell George you didn't want the job."

Jeff was remembering the look in Taine's eyes—the man *had* recognized him. But he had lied to Borman and to Avilla. Why? What did he want?

He shrugged. "I've changed my mind," he said. His voice was casual. "I can always get to Vera Cruz."

The suspicion deepened in Borman's eyes. "You don't

look like the sort of man who changes his mind often," he snapped. Then, pressing: "Get on that horse and get out of here!"

Jeff grinned faintly. Deliberately he drew his empty gun and without haste he reloaded.

Lounging against the corral bars, Nat Hines waited— his glance went from Jeff to Borman. . . .

Avilla waved him off. "I guess he's staying, Nat."

The gunman gave Jeff a slow, hard look, then sauntered off toward the bunkhouse.

One of the Mexican wagon drivers came up. He spoke to Avilla in Spanish. Where did Avilla want the wagons unloaded.

Borman answered, his voice clipped. "Leave the wagons right there! Don't unload them!"

The driver turned and motioned to the others . . . they moved away, toward the Mexican quarters.

Avilla said to Jeff: "If Mr. Taine hires you, you ride with me."

Jeff slipped his loaded gun back into his holster.

"Where?"

"Durango!"

Jeff nodded. He looked at Borman. "The roan's mine?"

Borman said coldly: "We'll talk about it later." He waited, watching Jeff as he turned, went into the bunkhouse.

Then, turning to Avilla, he said harshly: "He's trouble, Vince. You should have killed him right away, when you had the chance."

Avilla said: "We can always kill him." He looked to-

49

ward the house. "But George is right. We can always use another gun. Especially one like his."

Borman turned to the house. "George knows him, Vince." His voice was flat with conviction. "I wonder why he lied."

Vince shrugged. "Let's take a look at the guns."

The long square boxes were nailed closed and covered with tarpaulin. Borman pried open one of the boxes . . . the rifles were new Winchester repeaters, .30-30. The grease had been wiped from them.

"A hundred of them," Borman said. "And enough ammunition to wipe out an army." He grinned coldly. "There's your revolution, Vince."

Vincente reached down for one of the rifles. His eyes burned with a deep fire. "We'll be ready for General Franco, in Durango. . . ."

Borman put his hand on Avilla's, holding him. "The guns have been checked," he said. "No sense in wasting time and ammunition."

Avilla looked at him. "I do my own checking," he said. "Even if the guns are new."

Borman shrugged. "If you insist—"

He reached into the box, his hand sliding from the Winchester Avilla had been about to pick up to the one next to it. It had a small notch on the polished wood butt. He handed it to the boss of the *Amigos*.

Avilla pried open an ammunition box, scooped up a handful of shells, loaded the Winchester. He walked to the end of the corral, picked out a distant target on a

bare slope and fired rapidly. He was pleased at the results.

Borman watched him slide the rifle back into the long box, nail it shut.

"There's plenty of ammunition," he said casually. "But if all your men start checking out their gun—"

"I'm satisfied," Avilla said. "My men will save their ammunition for General Franco . . ."

He looked off toward the distant, desolate hills, his thoughts leaping into the future.

"If we win in Durango, Cass. . . ."

He did not see the look in Cass Borman's eyes . . . and it was well that he didn't. . . .

Jeff Corrin washed leisurely at the stand outside the bunkhouse. . . . he shaved and put on a clean shirt. No one bothered him. Several hard-eyed gunmen came out to look him over . . . they were a clannish group, these Americans, and it would take a while, Jeff thought, before he would be accepted by them.

Silent Gordon avoided him, acting as though Jeff were not here—but Jeff knew he'd have to watch this man. The others were neutral. If George Taine hired him he'd be just another gunslinger hired to do a job.

Thirty minutes later Jeff knocked on the door of the ranch house. Maria answered. She had changed into a house dress, but she was no more womanly because of it.

She eyed him quizzically for a moment, then motioned him inside.

"Father's waiting for you in the study. I'll take you to him."

Jeff followed her across a big living room dominated by a fieldstone fireplace to a carved oak door. Maria opened it and they went in.

George Taine had changed into a white linen suit, which was the way Jeff remembered him—big, important-looking. He was sitting at his desk, a drink at his elbow.

He said firmly: "Leave us, Maria!"

Maria hesitated, then closed the door behind her. Taine waved Jeff to a chair by the desk.

"You're a damned fool!" he said sharply.

Jeff, about to sit down, remained standing. His eyes narrowed.

"Oh, sit down!" the big man snapped. "If I was going to tell Borman and Avilla who you are I'd have told them before."

Jeff settled slowly into his chair.

"Why didn't you?"

The big man ignored the question. "You looking for that *New York World* correspondent, Roger Briscole?"

"Not particularly."

George Taine frowned. "Then why is Jeff Corrin here? The Rangers have no authority in Mexico."

Jeff leaned forward. "Someone killed my brother, Ben. In a border town called Ansara." Taine's slight head nod indicated he knew the place. "Ben was killed while talking to a man who came in to file a story to the

New York World—a man who claimed he was Roger Briscole."

George Taine's hand tightened on his glass. "Cass never said—" He cut himself off, raised the glass to his lips, his eyes hard, judging Jeff.

"Didn't you leave the Rangers? Forced to resign, as I remember?"

Jeff nodded.

"Then you don't care about what goes on here . . . Avilla's revolution . . . or Roger Briscole? You just want the man who killed your brother?"

Jeff leaned forward in his chair. "What is going on here, Mr. Taine? Besides illegal gun-running?"

George's voice was curt. "Nothing that concerns you—or," his eyes turned bitter, "anything you can help with."

He got up and started to pace behind his desk. He looked drawn now, uncertain.

"Who killed Ben?"

The big man stopped by the edge of the desk, looked at Jeff. "I'm afraid you'll have to find out for yourself. I wasn't there."

"Who sent that wire story for Briscole?"

George Taine hesitated, then said bitterly: "There's nothing you can do, Jeff. You're trapped here—like I am . . ." He paused, listening for a moment, then walked quickly to the study window and closed the inside shutters. It was suddenly gloomy in the big room. He stood there a moment, a dark shadow of a man . . . then, turning to Jeff: "It wouldn't do you any good if you knew . . ."

Jeff asked him, "Who's Cass Borman?"

Taine shrugged. "A man I wish I had never met." He walked back to his desk, sat down . . . Jeff's eyes were becoming accustomed to the change in light. He saw Taine settle back in the chair—he looked suddenly old and worried and less important than he had seemed.

"An adventurer," Taine went on slowly . . . "charming when he wants to be . . . a good manager, but a man without . . ." He paused and the bitterness sharpened in his voice. "Look, who am I to talk about Cass Borman? I went in with him with open eyes. It was his idea to take over this place. A good base, he said, for—"

"Stolen cattle?" Jeff said.

"Contraband," Taine answered. "Stolen and illegal goods, bought for a fraction of their value." He leaned forward across the desk. "I'm a big man in Texas, as you know. And my ranch, the Triangle T, ends at the Mexican border. No one checks my wagons when I cross. . . ."

Jeff nodded. "So that's what made you rich?"

"And Cass Borman powerful," Taine answered.

"What about Avilla?"

Taine shrugged. "I married his sister when he was just a wild young man away at school. Avilla is . . . a misguided man. Cass figured we could use his revolution . . . use Avilla and his small band to divert the Mexican authorities who were getting suspicious. If Mexican troops spend their time chasing the *Amigos*, they won't have time to interfere with us."

Jeff walked back to the desk. He studied the big

man for a moment. "You have that correspondent locked up here?"

Taine nodded. "Technically he's a guest . . . he's covering Avilla's revolution."

"But it's Cass Borman who files his stories?"

Taine nodded again.

Jeff put his hands on the desk, leaned toward the big man. "All right, you've got yourself in a jam, Mr. Taine. That's not my concern. And even if it was, I have no authority to do anything about it." He paused, his eyes hard. "I want the man who killed my brother!"

Taine said heavily: "I told you I didn't know anyone was killed at Ansara."

"Who went with Borman?"

Taine pulled away from the anger in Jeff's gaze. "Gordon, Nogales, Eaton . . ." He shrugged. "Any of them could have." He shook his head. "I didn't see Cass leave."

Jeff straightened, his eyes bitter. "You own this ranch, you said—"

"But Cass runs it," Taine interrupted. "You'll have to believe me . . ." He stood up, glanced toward the window. "If I could get back across the border—"

"You just came back from Durango," Jeff reminded him. "Why didn't you just keep going?"

"Four of Cass' men rode with me," Taine answered grimly. "If I had turned north with those guns I would have been shot."

He put his gaze on Jeff. "That's the way it is, Jeff. I'm as much a prisoner here as Roger Briscole."

"How about your daughter?" Jeff said. "She rides—"

"With her uncle Vincente," Taine cut in harshly. "Besides, she doesn't know what I've been doing with Cass —and I don't want her to know. That's what keeps her alive, Jeff—her not knowing . . ."

He walked to the table and poured himself another drink. "She's all for the revolution—" He turned, glass in hand. "I couldn't care less."

"And Avilla?"

"He's got his guns now . . . he'll be marching to Durango." He drank slowly, his eyes hard. "I have a very strong feeling he won't be coming back."

Jeff turned, walked slowly to the door.

Taine said: "Jeff . . ." and when the younger man turned he added softly, "Neither will you." He held up his half empty glass. "Cass holds all the cards. I found that out too late."

Jeff said grimly: "Don't be too sure, Mr. Taine. I'm a hard man to kill." He walked out then, leaving the big man standing in a pall of gloom and depression.

VIII

THE LATE afternoon sun slanted across the trees ringing the ranch and a wind stirred, bringing a mock feeling of relief from the brutal heat of the day.

The Americans dozed on their bunks for the most part. A few, stripped to the waist, played a lack-

luster game of cards around a table set by the door to catch the breeze.

Silent Gordon came into the bunkhouse. . . . Jeff was by his bunk, watching the card game. The *segundo* paused a moment, eyeing him, then walked over.

"You're riding with us tomorrow, Galahad. That roan you picked out will be your mount—it'll come out of your wages."

Jeff said: "What kind of wages?"

"Same as the rest of us," Gordon said, "two hundred a month." He turned to the others who had paused in what they were doing—they were waiting to hear what Gordon had to say.

"You all heard me," Gordon said. "We're going to Durango." He grinned crookedly. "I expect this time we'll earn our money."

A man with an old face stirred, sat up slowly on his bunk. He had a sinewy, tough body and he kept a skin tight glove on his right hand, eating or sleeping. It could have been an affectation, a bit of showmanship to draw attention to the fact that he was a professional —a man who lived by his gun. In actuality it was to cover burn-scarred fingers.

His hair was red and it was known he had been born somewhere in Texas, near the Brazos river—he was called Brazos Red. No one knew his real name and he never told.

"Whose idea, Silent?"

Gordon didn't answer him right away. He said instead:

"Anybody got any letters to write, write them now." He paused. "Not all of us will be riding back—"

"*Whose idea?*"

Brazos' voice didn't raise, but it carried a hard and arresting emphasis and now Gordon turned to him.

"Mr. Borman," he said. And there was a subtle challenge in his tone which Jeff noticed. These two men, he reflected, didn't get along.

Brazos Red eased back on his bunk. "Long as it's not that goddam Mex's show!" He fished a long thin black cigar from his shirt pocket hanging on a corner of his bunk, stuck it into a corner of his mouth.

"We heard George Franco is coming north with a hundred troopers. We gonna hoorah Durango before he gets there?"

"We're gonna wait for him in Durango," Gordon said, and a cold light flickered in his gaze as he saw the match in Brazos' hand stop short of the cigar.

"*Wait for him?*" Brazos swung his legs over the side of the bunk and stood up.

Gordon nodded.

"Avilla and his men will be ready just outside of town. We help him beat that Mex general and we get a bonus —a thousand dollars apiece. Mister Borman's orders."

Brazos shrugged. "Guess who'll do most of the fighting," he muttered. He lighted up. He didn't have much use for Avilla's brand of revolutionaries.

Jeff turned, started for the door.

Gordon's hard voice bit at him. "Where you going, Galahad?"

Jeff looked at him. "I don't have any letters to write."
He went outside.

Gordon called after him. "Just be around, ready to ride, in the morning." His voice was ugly as he said it.

Jeff paused outside, by the wash stand, to roll himself a cigarette.

Brazos walked out after him, puffing on his cigar. He watched Jeff for a moment, then: "New man . . . you just come in?"

Jeff nodded.

"What'ud you do to Silent?"

Jeff struck a match, lighted his smoke. He didn't say anything and his face revealed nothing.

Brazos grinned coldly. "He doesn't like me, either. He'll kill you, first chance he gets."

"He'll try," Jeff said.

Brazos looked him over slowly. "Well, you talk tough. Like most kids . . ."

He leaned against the bunkhouse wall and brought his gloved right hand slowly up in front of him.

Jeff's eyes followed it, wondering.

"My maw died when I was still sucking milk," Brazos said. His voice was casual, as though Jeff had asked him and he was bored telling it. "There were seven more of us, all older than me—all of us hungry, all of us runny-nosed. My paw picked cotton, chopped wood and made coffins on the side, to feed us. One day he was called in to work on the gin. He was new at it and

he got his hand caught in something . . . don't know what. Tore most of his hand off . . .

"The doctor had to cut him free. Did a nice job. Arm healed around a stump of a hand. But Pa never picked cotton again. Fact is—(Brazos was slowly squeezing his gloved hand into a fist, then loosening it again) he never did a lick of work after that."

Jeff cut in with a trace of impatience. "Sounds like a long story. If you don't mind—"

"*Wait!*"

The word was shot at Jeff as from a rifle . . . Jeff, turning away, paused.

Brazos' gun hand flexed again. "I haven't finished." He took his cigar from his mouth, spat out bits of tobacco, clamped his teeth on it again.

"I was there when the doc cut my paw's hand off. Saw the way he worked. Guess that's when I decided I wanted to be like him—a doctor. Paw wasn't so much to me anymore . . . that doc took his place. I followed him around like a dog . . . finally he said when I growed to fifteen I could work with him . . ."

Brazos paused. Jeff waited, somehow compelled to listen, feeling a strange and distorted need in this man to tell his story.

"See this hand?" Brazos said, holding out his gloved fist. "Got it burned one night, trying to save my paw. Lying dead drunk in a stall, he was. Damn fool set fire to himself with an old pipe, and didn't even know it . . ."

He shook his head slowly, his eyes dark with some

deep inner sympathy for himself. "Man can't be a sur-
geon with a hand like this, can he?" he asked rhetori-
cally. "But . . . take a good look at it, Galahad . . ."

His outstretched hand jerked and disappeared and
suddenly there was his gun in it . . . the draw was
incredibly fast and Jeff tensed, his stomach muscles
tightening under the deadly menace of that leveled gun.

Brazos Red chuckled coldly. "Just don't go getting
any ideas about old Brazos here."

He turned abruptly then and strode back into the
bunkhouse.

Jeff watched him, eyes still lidded, shocked—his stomach muscles relaxing slowly.

He was turning away when Nogales Smith came outside. The cherubic-faced outlaw grinned.

"Whatsamatter, Galahad? Brazos shake you up?"

Jeff looked at him. "Is he that way all the time?"

Nogales nodded. "Pulls that story an' trick on all the
new men." He moved toward Jeff, taking a bite from a
chaw of tobacco. "Hell of it is nobody around here is
near as fast with a hand gun. Gordon can shoot rings
around him with a rifle—but even he doesn't cross Brazos Red."

Jeff looked toward the bunkhouse.

"You been here long?"

"Longer than most," Nogales said. "Brazos was here
first—couple of other men, too. Both of them are dead
—Nick was killed yesterday—you heard Mr. Taine tell it."
He spat juice into the dirt by the washstand. "The pay's
good, but the turnover is bad . . ."

Jeff said casually: "Who does the hiring—Taine or Cass Borman?"

Nogales shrugged. "Borman, usually. Least that's the way it was with us—me, Gordon, Cobb and Nat. We were headed for Vera Cruz, too, but stopped over in Durango. Got into a little trouble over a couple of local girls and wound up in the goddam Mexican clink. Cass —Mr. Borman—did some local bribing and got us out. Five minutes later we were working for him."

He looked off toward the bunkhouse, then back to Jeff, his voice lowering. "How much did you get, Galahad?"

Jeff eyed him, frowning.

Nogales wiped a trickle of tobacco juice from his chin with the back of his hand.

"Look, Galahad . . . no one comes across the Mexican border these days for his health."

Jeff considered. It would be to his advantage to keep the myth going that he was on the run from Texas law.

He shrugged. "Near thirty thousand. I didn't make an exact count."

Nogales whistled softly. "No wonder you wanted a horse and a run into Vera Cruz. A man could live out the rest of his life on that anywhere in South America."

"I don't have it with me," Jeff cut in coldly.

"Of course not," Nogales said, grinning. "I never figgered you for a fool." He chewed on his tobacco cud for a moment, thinking . . . this had been in the back of his mind for a while anyway.

"Tell you what, Galahad," he said, his voice conspir-

atorial, "cut me in for half and I'll help you get it." He shot another glance back to the bunkhouse. "I was getting ready to pull stakes anyway. Pay's good, like I said—but somehow I always end up broke by the end of the month." He mused a moment . . . "Cards, women . . ." he shrugged. "An' this new job coming up—tangling with this Mex general and a hundred troopers ain't like raiding a few border towns. Going into Durango ain't gonna be too healthy—"

"I'll take my chances," Jeff said shortly.

He started to leave.

Nogales said coldly: "Better think about it, Galahad. I know this part of Mexico. And I also know what they're planning—about you."

Jeff swung back to him.

"Who?"

"Borman and Gordon."

Jeff waited; then, impatient, "What are they planning?"

Nogales' grin was that of a man who had hooked his fish. "One third of what you've got hidden out there somewhere?"

Jeff made a show of reluctance.

"Aw, come on, Galahad," Nogales wheedled. "Twenty thousand dollars is still a lot of *dinero* in South America."

Jeff nodded, his eyes grim.

Nogales said: "Is it a deal?"

Jeff's voice was grim: "You better know your way around out there, if we're going to make it to Vera Cruz."

Nogales grinned. "That's my job. You just stay alive, Galahad." He glanced toward the ranch house. "Borman's orders—soon as the fighting starts in Durango, Gordon kills you."

He turned back to Jeff. "We cut out just before, Galahad. I'll have the horses ready. Gordon'll have his hands full with them Mex soldiers . . ."

"Thanks," Jeff said. Then, as Nogales started to leave: "Just one more thing, Smith. Who went down to Ansara with Borman a few days ago?"

Nogales studied him for a beat, then: "Gordon," he said.

IX

THE CANDLE-LIGHTED dining room had been designed in another era when life had been simpler and times less troublesome. The long oak table seated twelve and at one time this had been the usual attendance . . . now four people were clustered at one end, their voices muted.

George Taine sat at the head of the table. Maria and Avilla were on his left—Borman sat on his right.

The Mexican servants moved silently and unobtrusively from the kitchen and back, but none appeared very hungry.

Avilla appeared lost in thought . . . he was thinking of Durango.

Borman toyed with his wine glass. He was watching Taine covertly, studying the big man. The strain between them had been growing for some time now . . . he had known it would happen, and he had prepared for it.

He lifted his glass now, looked at Avilla. "Here's to Durango," he toasted, "and to a new order in Mexico."

Avilla's eyes came up to him, startled.

Maria said impulsively, "To Uncle Vincente," and lifted her glass, her smile bright. "After Durango all of northern Mexico will be behind you."

Avilla shrugged. "But first—Durango." He lifted his glass to his lips, but his eyes were thoughtful and his voice troubled.

Borman smiled coldly. "You seem unsure—"

Avilla looked at him across the table, his eyes dark and faintly bitter. "In a battle no one can be sure."

Borman leaned back in his chair. "This is a hell of a time to have doubts, Vince." His voice hardened. "We got you the guns you wanted—twelve of our men will be fighting with you. We've committed ourselves, Vince—you've got to win in Durango!"

Maria said quickly: "Of course we'll win!" But her gaze went from Avilla to her father, searching for assurance.

Avilla said softly: "Only twelve of your gunfighters, Cass—?"

"Thirteen," Borman answered, glancing at Taine. "You did hire Galahad?"

Taine shrugged. "Why not? We've been hiring his kind for years."

Cass Borman turned back to Avilla. "I'm keeping Brazos Red and a couple of men here. Just in case—"

Avilla's grin was crooked, cold. "I see that you, also, have doubts." He straightened in his chair and took a deep breath. "Perhaps it is normal to have doubts on the eve of battle." He lifted his glass again, his eyes bright. "Well—here's to Durango—and the revolution!"

Taine put his glass down as he saw Roger Briscole appear in the dining room doorway . . . he was facing in that direction and saw him first.

"Glad you changed your mind, Roger," he said and the others turned to look at the *World* correspondent. Taine waved him to a chair beside Borman. "I was beginning to doubt my own hospitality."

Roger walked over and sat in the chair next to Cass, but he did not look at him.

Borman said indifferently: "He's been on somewhat of a hunger strike while you were gone, George."

The newspaper man watched as one of the servants poured wine into his glass.

"Captivity is hardly conducive to good eating," he murmured.

Maria frowned. "I was not aware that you were being held here against your will." She looked questioningly at her father.

Taine shrugged. "Far as I'm concerned Mr. Briscole can leave any time."

"Of course," Borman cut in smoothly, "We couldn't guarantee his safety, once he left the confines of the ranch."

Roger smiled faintly. "You could, if you wanted to."

Maria was disconcerted. "You've been our guest. I was not informed you felt yourself a prisoner, although I understood you are not in sympathy with the revolution." She looked directly at her father.

"When are you going back to the Texas ranch?"

Taine considered a moment before answering. "Soon," he said.

"Mr. Briscole could go with you," Maria suggested.

Taine eyed Borman, a small smile on his lips. "Of course," he said to his daughter.

Borman didn't say anything.

Roger's gaze moved back and forth between the two men. He smiled faintly. "I'll hold you to it, Mr. Taine."

It was dark outside the bunkhouse when Jeff paused by the well which was enclosed by a lattice-framed structure and interlaced by grape vines.

He lounged in the shadows, smoking, thinking of tomorrow, reassessing his course of action. He knew who had killed Ben, and this is what he had come for—nothing more.

In Durango, he would kill Gordon. And then—well, there was nothing back in Texas for him. And Vera Cruz was as good a place as any. . . .

He didn't see Maria until she loomed up . . . he butted out his cigarette and turned to her and she stopped, momentarily startled. Then: "Oh, it's you, Galahad."

Her laughter was soft and pleasant. "I didn't expect anyone here. . . ."

He said quickly, "I'll leave."

"No—stay." She moved up closer and while there was no moon there was enough starlight for him to see her face.

"I'm curious," she said. "Galahad? That isn't your real name, of course."

He shook his head. He didn't particularly like this woman and he didn't want to get involved in a conversation with her.

But she wasn't about to let go.

"Did you kill anyone?"

He nodded.

"Is that why you're wanted by the American law?"

He said coldly, "I reckon that's none of your business, Miss Taine."

She reacted angrily for a moment, then, surprisingly: "You're right, it isn't." She glanced toward the quiet, darkened bunkhouse. "Most of those men in there, hired by my father and Cass, are the same. But, at least they're fighting for a good cause now . . ."

"Whose cause?"

"The people of Mexico!" There was conviction in her voice.

His tone was cynical: "The *Amigos?*"

"My uncle's revolution. My father supports it. First

68

the provinces of Chihuahua and Sonora—then all of Mexico."

He shook his head. "Raiding small border settlements . . . hit and run . . . killing people that have nothing to do with your revolution . . . who want nothing of anyone but the chance to make a living—"

"That's not true!"

Jeff shrugged. "When was the last time you were back in Texas?"

She was silent then, looking off toward the darkened hills. "I haven't been there."

He eyed her, curious. "You mean you've grown up here without ever wanting to go into Texas . . . to be part of your father's life there?"

"My mother was Mexican," she said slowly. "I went to school in Guadalajara. My mother's relatives are here . . . my uncle Vincente . . ."

"Your father is a big man in Texas." He was frowning, trying to remember what little he knew of George Taine. There had never been any mention of a daughter connected with publicity about him.

Her voice gave her away. "I'm Mexican," she said. "Texas was our land once . . . it was taken away, by force . . ."

She paused. "You're a Texan?"

He nodded.

"You want to go back?"

"Some day."

She looked at him a long moment. "Maybe I will, too. With my father . . . after the revolution. . . ."

X

THE SUN's first rays bathed the ruins of the old presidio across the river in soft pink light . . . they came stealing down the stratified walls of the mesa, probing with weightless fingers the quiet trees that lined and surrounded the *Paseo Grande* ranch.

In the yard the riders were mounted and ready, waiting for Vincente Avilla. The wagons, loaded with ammunition and rifles, were hitched and ready to roll.

Jeff sat astride the big roan, flanked by Nogales Smith on one side and Gordon on the other. Thirteen hired guns . . . all of them Americans . . . all of them (except Jeff) outlaws.

Jeff glanced along the mounted line . . . hard men, faces closed, emotionless . . . some with cigarettes dangling from tight lips. This was what they had hired on for . . . they didn't give a damn about Avilla's revolution, Jeff thought . . . they were being paid by Cass Borman and they took orders. Fighting General Franco and his troopers was just another gun job. . . .

But sitting there, waiting, Jeff had the uneasy feeling that this thing for which Avilla had waited so long was going to backfire . . . he felt it, like he felt the prickle at the back of his neck.

The *Amigos'* boss came out of the ranch house, dressed

for travel. With him were Maria, Cass, George Taine—and a man Jeff recognized only from description—Roger Briscole.

They paused on the wide veranda. Maria was dressed for riding . . . there was a determined look on her face. Avilla glanced at the waiting men, then back to Taine's daughter.

"I'd rather you didn't come this time, Maria," he said. He looked at Taine. "Make her stay home, George . . ."

Taine smiled faintly as Maria turned to him, a cold look in her eyes. "You want me to put chains on her, Vince?" He looked at Maria then, and there was concern in his voice. "I've never told you what to do, Maria . . . maybe I should have . . ." He took a deep breath. "Don't go to Durango this time—"

She cut him off. "I have friends in Durango—I'll be staying with them."

"This isn't the same," her father said sharply. "General Franco has field guns . . . no one will be safe in Durango."

She shook her head, unaffected by his wishes; she had never been close to her father.

"Even General Franco won't use those guns to kill helpless people in town."

Cass intervened, his voice grim: "Don't be too sure, Maria—"

She turned sharply to him: "I won't even discuss it with you, Cass!"

He reddened slightly, but held his temper. "I'm only thinking of your safety, Maria. For Vince and these

71

men . . . well, it's their job and your uncle's revolution. But why risk your neck—"

"It's my revolution, too," she said curtly. "I want to be in Durango when Uncle Vince raises his banner over the town square."

There was no keeping her behind and those men on the veranda knew it. Avilla glanced at George Taine and said simply: "I'll guard her with my life, George."

Taine looked at his daughter for a long regretful moment . . . he saw the gulf between them . . . the gap he had unconsciously let grow and he knew it was too late for words . . . maybe too late for anything.

He said quietly, "Good luck, Maria," and turned and went into the house.

Roger Briscole made a sudden decision. "Let me ride with you, too, Avilla."

Cass' voice was cold. "No."

Roger glanced at him. "Last night you said I could leave any time I wanted to. Are you backing out now? Am I really a prisoner here?"

Maria had stopped at the foot of the stairs; she turned to look at Borman, frowning. "If he wants to, let him come, Cass."

Cass hesitated. "I guess it's really up to your uncle, Maria . . . if he wants to be saddled with a foreign correspondent who isn't exactly favorable—"

Roger cut in quickly, turning to Avilla: "Maybe I was wrong about you . . . your revolution. Let me go to Durango and find out."

Avilla shook his head. "You'll be in the way."

Roger appealed to Maria. "I'll stay with Miss Taine."

Avilla considered. If he won he'd need a good press in the United States. This man could give it to him.

He shrugged. "I can't guarantee your safety, Mr. Briscole."

Roger smiled. "I'll take my chances."

Avilla looked at Cass. Borman waved casually. "Good luck, Vince. . . ."

He watched Roger and the girl take their places on the seats of separate wagons. Avilla mounted the horse waiting for him at the tie rail . . . he glanced back to Borman once and Cass waved again . . . and then they moved out of the yard toward the desolate hills beyond. . . .

There was a wagon road of sorts to Durango from the *Paseo Grande* ranch, but Avilla and his contingent left it at noon, heading south, following an old stream bed in which scoured and whitened rocks reflected the glaring sun. The arid hills moved in on them, rocky and steep-sided, from which chuckwallas and collared lizards watched with beady-eyed interest. . . .

The mounted men were divided into two contingents —half of them, led by Avilla, riding forward of the wagons—the others, with Gordon in the forefront, riding behind.

Jeff rode loose in the saddle, relaxed, his eyes lidded. Almost as soon as they had left the wagon road Gordon had dropped back so that he was riding almost alone

behind the rear group of riders . . . and Jeff could feel the killer's eyes on him, alert and watchful.

Gordon was taking no chances that Jeff would slip away. . . .

The ancient dry creek meandered between the hills. Here and there small algae-covered pools of water appeared, close to the banks, protected from the drying blaze of the sun by overhanging mesquite or cholla.

Finally, at a turn in one of the innumerable bends of the *arroyo* a spot of light flashed across Avilla's path. It moved back and forth, a reflection of the sun, man-directed.

Avilla raised his right hand . . . the riders and the wagons behind him halted.

High up on the slope above the creek a man in ant-hill sombrero and crossed bandolier appeared. He waved his rifle in signal to the men below. . . . Avilla waved back.

They rode on now, and ahead of them the river banks grew trees, mostly cottonwoods and some willows, an occasional live oak. And there was water now under the horses and the wagons, shallow but running.

The walls of an old mission church, abandoned, its walls crumbling, came into view . . . then a dozen or so adobe huts. Once, a long time ago, Father Kingo had built this mission and this town, Santa Lucia, one of a string of missions the padre had built in what was then called the *Pimeria Alta*. Now this settlement was forgotten even by those in power in Mexico City. . . .

This was the hideout of Avilla's *Amigos* when they

were not raiding . . . a motley group of men of all ages, bound by a common cause, a hatred of the men in power in Mexico City, and a strong loyalty to Vincente Avilla. Most of them had a price on their head . . . most of them would be promptly hanged if caught by Federal troops.

They had their women here, their children—they lived without a future and only a burning, bitter hope.

A giant of a man, bearded, bare-chested, holding an old single shot Krag rifle came out to meet Avilla. The others, men, women and children straggled behind. He embraced the *Amigos'* boss, lifting him off the ground, while the others looked on.

"You have the guns, Vincente?" he asked, and it was a desperate cry . . . "you have the guns . . . ?"

Avilla broke free of the other's embrace, grinned. "In the wagons, Tomas. Guns for everyone."

Tomas turned, waved to his men. They ran to the wagons, hauled out the rifle boxes and ammunition cases . . . they cried and laughed like children at the shiny new Winchester repeaters, the boxes of shells.

The guns were quickly handed out, the bandoliers filled. Avilla gave orders to Tomas. "There will be no useless firing, Tomas . . . no wasting of ammunition. Tomorrow we ride to Durango."

Tomas nodded. He turned and bellowed Avilla's orders to the men, then turned back to Avilla.

"It is true? We hear that General Franco is marching on Durango . . . ?"

Avilla nodded. "With a hundred troopers—the pride of Mexico City."

Tomas grinned. "And we, Vincente?"

"We'll be there, waiting for him."

Tomas' big hand tightened on the stock of his new Winchester. "The *Americanos*—they will fight?"

Avilla smiled coldly. "They'll be in Durango—with me. They have been promised a bonus—for money, *si*, Tomas, they will fight."

He put a hand on Tomas' powerful shoulder. "You will lead your men. You will be waiting outside of town . . . in the old *arroyo* that cuts south of the Mesa Blanca . . . When General Franco attacks the town you will attack him—from behind."

Tomas rubbed his palm lovingly over his rifle. "I can't wait, Vincente! After all these years . . . that fat pig, Franco . . ."

"He will have a hundred soldiers," Avilla warned. "They are trained to fight. It will not be easy."

Tomas shrugged. "Come . . . you camp here tonight . . . no?"

Avilla nodded. "We leave early in the morning."

Tomas turned and signaled to the women behind him. "We eat well tonight, Vincente."

Then his gaze brushed over the mounted men . . . they were eyeing Tomas and Avilla and the ragged group of revolutionaries, aloof, cold. Tomas sensed their faint contempt and anger made its brief flare in his eyes and then faded.

He turned back to Avilla, smiling, bitter: "A half

dozen of your brother-in-law's steers, Vincente. For to-night's barbecue. He has so many . . . we didn't think he'd mind . . ."

Avilla shrugged.

Walking toward them, Maria said: "No, my father doesn't mind, Tomas."

Tomas looked past Avilla, seeing Maria for the first time now. He swept his hat from his head. "Maria . . . I . . ."

She was smiling. "It is good to see you again, Tomas," she said.

Tomas picked her up, hugged her.

Maria gasped, laughing: "You're crushing my ribs, To-mas . . ."

He put her down, held her at arm's length, glad to see her. Then, soberly: "Why are you here?"

"I'm going to Durango with you," she said.

Tomas glanced at Avilla . . . Avilla shrugged.

Maria said: "Oh, don't look so uncomfortable, Tomas. I won't be in the way." She glanced toward the huts. "I'd like to wash . . . chat with your wife, Felicia. . . ."

She left them.

Tomas looked up at the waiting, mounted men. "Please," he said quietly . . . "make yourselves comfortable. We will eat soon . . . we will celebrate . . ."

XI

THE BIG COOKING fires lighted up the shadows of the
old village. The ruined church, its cross and its bell
tower gone, seemed to look sadly upon the scene, remembering with what hopes Father Kingo had built it
and to what low estate it had now fallen.

A half dozen carcasses of Paseo Grande beef turned
slowly on stout pole spits, basted and presided over
by the women of the village. Pots of beans simmered
on the fire and there was laughter from the men, smiles
from the women and happy play from the children.

It was celebration time for the *Amigos* . . . but for
many of these rough Mexican peasants, Jeff thought,
this could be their last good meal. . . .

Here, as at the *Paseo Grande* ranch, the American
gunslingers did not mix with the Mexicans. They lined
up before one of the spits and took their portions of
beans and beef and went off together—a group apart,
faintly contemptuous, arrogantly sure of their superiority.

Jeff, too, felt a distance between himself and these
men . . . he was apart from the revolution and whatever these people felt. Whatever social justice they
might have on their side, was none of his business.

But he was being forced into doing some rethinking
concerning Avilla and these men who waited to ride

against General Franco tomorrow. The *Amigos* who had been raiding the Texas border towns and who therefore were generally hated, were not the bandits he had expected. Maybe they had been misled into thinking the raids were necessary—a way of stirring up resentment and interest in their plight—a way, too, of obtaining money and food and guns, for the Lord knew there was little enough of these in the Mexican villages of Sonora and Chihuahua.

Jeff was hunkered down with his plate of barbecued beef and beans when Nogales joined him. The small man glanced at the Mexicans by the fires and voiced the thought shared by his companions.

"They'll cut an' run when General Franco's field guns open up on them . . ."

Jeff shrugged. "Maybe. . . ."

Nogales said: "Hell, I know them. They don't like us, not one goddam bit. But they need us . . ."

He started to hunker down beside Jeff, then thought of something. "Can't eat this stuff without havin' something to drink." He set his plate down beside Jeff. "I'll see what I can steal for us. . . ."

He walked off into the shadows.

Jeff looked toward the fire . . . Maria was helping Tomas' wife serve. He saw Roger Briscole's tall figure loom up and receive his plate . . . the correspondent said something to Maria and she smiled, then shook her head and Briscole turned toward the wagons.

He paused, plate in hand . . . he seemed out of place here, and he was. But his aloofness was not racial, Jeff

guessed—he didn't belong with either group of these men and he knew it.

He saw Jeff then, eating alone, and he walked over, hesitating a moment before saying: "Mind if I join you?"

Jeff made a gesture that indicated he didn't care. Roger squatted down beside him, but it was apparent that he was more used to sitting at dinner tables and after a few uncomfortable moments he got up and found an empty ammunition case which he brought back by Jeff and used as a seat.

"I'm Roger Briscole," he said. "I'm a newspaperman, covering this revolution."

Jeff didn't say anything.

Roger picked at his beans, but he was not really interested in eating.

"You look familiar, somehow," he said. "But I'm sure we haven't met . . . or have we?"

Jeff said coldly: "We haven't."

Briscole took the rebuff and was silent for a moment. Then: "What do you think of them?" he asked, indicating Avilla and his *Amigos* with his chin. "Have they got a chance against General Franco?"

"I'm not being paid to think," Jeff answered curtly.

Roger said coldly, "Just to kill . . ." He stood up, knowing he wasn't wanted here. But he took one last look at Jeff. "Sorry if I bothered you. But you do remind me of someone I met before I crossed the border. In Austin, I think . . . Texas Ranger headquarters . . ."

He was talking about Ben, Jeff knew . . . there was a

strong family resemblance. He didn't want this man to pursue it.

"Maybe," he said harshly, "on a wanted poster."

Nogales Smith came up with a bottle and this decided things for Roger—he moved away, toward the wagons.

Nogales hunkered down beside Jeff and set his bottle down on the ammunition case Roger had brought up.

"Pulque," he said. "Made by Mex, tastes like Mex . . . but what the hell, it gives you a solid feeling in the gut a man needs just before a fight."

He looked off toward Roger melting into the shadows. "What'ud he want?"

"Company, I guess," Jeff answered. He shook his head to the pulque bottle offered by Nogales.

The runty outlaw took a long swig, wiped his lips. His voice lowered. "We'll cut out tomorrow—soon as we can. I've got two good pack animals picked out, a couple of extra canteens. We'll need them to cross the desert . . ."

Jeff was barely listening . . . he was watching Maria by the fire, remembering last night. She did not know what she was getting into . . .

Nogales' voice cut into his thoughts.

"How much time you figger we'll need to get to where you cached the money? Two days? Three?"

"From Durango?"

Nogales nodded.

"Two days at most," Jeff said.

Nogales chuckled. "We'll fool them." He glanced to-

ward Gordon, who was with the rest of his men. "Gordon will figger we'll head for Vera Cruz, or Tampico. But we'll go west instead, Galahad. There's a small fishing village on the west coast of Mexico—a place called Guaymas—"

He paused as one of the longriders came by. Nat Hines paused, looked down at Nogales, said: "Where'ud you hijack the bottle of pulque, Smith?"

Nogales pointed. "Church. They got a mess of them stacked up in the old wine cellar."

Nat Hines looked back toward his group. "Hey!" he said loudly. "I've found out where they keep the booze!"

Several men joined him—they moved off quickly toward the church.

Jeff let his gaze wander to Briscole, standing alone by one of the wagons.

"That correspondent," he said, "how does he get his stories back to his paper?"

Nogales grinned. "Cass Borman does it for him."

"Borman?"

Nogales wiped his gravy-stained mouth with the back of his hand. "Sure. Gordon goes along, just to make sure nothing goes wrong."

Jeff was silent a moment, trying to pin down a discontent within him. Ben had been killed trying to find out what happened to the *New York World* correspondent.

He glanced toward Roger Briscole, a shadow by the wagon. Damn it, Jeff thought, I don't owe that man

anything. But he owed his brother more than just getting his killer—he owed Ben what Ben had started out to do.

Find out who was behind the *Amigos*.

And that man was Cass Borman!

XII

GEORGE TAINE looked out his window at the night and he realized how Roger Briscole must have felt as one of Cass' men paused outside to light a cigarette.

Brazos Red was not overt in his watch of Taine's bedroom, but his presence was nonetheless real and Taine knew full well he was now a prisoner in his own house.

He picked up the brandy decanter and poured himself a drink and as he sipped it he reviewed his mistakes . . . the most bitter being his tieing up with Cass Borman.

George Taine did not excuse himself . . . he saw himself clearly for what he was . . . an opportunist, a man who had grabbed at money which meant power in any language and in any country.

He had thought he could handle Borman and outfox him . . . he was the one who had eventually been outfoxed.

He had married Maria's mother for the ranch she

owned here, not for love, although he had been tender to her and never mean. When Maria came along he had been glad to send her off to school . . . by then he had seen, with the help of Borman, a way to make his small holdings in Texas grow through contraband and stolen cattle . . . looting the small ranches on both sides of the border.

He was a big man now. He claimed dinner invitations at the governor's mansion . . . he was an honorary Captain in the Texas Rangers . . . and he had nothing.

He finished his drink and turned at the knock on his door, expecting it, wondering why it had taken Cass so long to come to him.

Borman walked slowly to the table by the window and poured himself a drink. He turned and looked at Taine and held up his glass:

"Here's to Vince's revolution, George."

Taine kept his glass in his hand, turning it slowly between his fingers.

"He's not going to make it, is he, Cass?"

Borman shrugged.

"I thought you were in love with my daughter." Taine's voice was bitter.

"I am," Cass replied. His voice was casual, his eyes studying Taine.

"Love—or want?" Taine said. "There is a difference, Cass."

Borman smiled. "Not to me."

Taine saw Brazos Red outside the window . . . a chill

went through him. But the gunman took a long drag on his cigarette, then moved away.

"You let her go to Durango," Taine said. "If you loved her you would have stopped her."

"That was your job," Cass said. He took a long sip of his brandy, then looked at Taine, considering something.

He smiled. "Tell me, George—how much is Maria worth to you?"

Taine searched Borman's face, trying to find a clue to the man's thoughts.

"I've got a half interest in this place—and in the Triangle T. But we've never put anything down on paper, have we, George?"

He looked down at his brandy glass, slowly sloshed the liquid around.

"Something happen to you, George, and I'm left out in the cold . . ."

Taine felt the chill reach down his spine.

"Let's put it this way," Cass continued. "Your daughter is in trouble. She's in Durango with Avilla, and General Franco won't give her any special favors. If she isn't shot, she'll get twenty years in prison, at least. And you know what a Mexican prison is like—"

Taine said harshly: "If Franco wins!"

Cass turned and set his glass down on the table. "He'll win."

Taine took a deep breath to smother the sinking feeling inside him. "You made sure?"

Cass nodded. "Every move." His smile was serene,

confident. "I got Vince his guns. *You* picked them up for him . . . that way he trusts you . . . and if something goes wrong he'll blame you—"

"Something will go wrong, of course!"

Borman laughed. "Of course. Only one out of every five of those new Winchesters will fire. And the ammunition—" His shrug told it all.

Taine looked at him, contempt in his eyes. "Why, Cass? That's what I want to know—*why?*"

"*We* used him!" Borman snapped. "You were in it with me, all the way!"

It was the truth, and George Taine turned away, his face crumbling.

"All right," he whispered. "I knew Vince never had a chance. But . . . this way. . . ."

He turned and looked bitterly at Cass. "It's mass murder!"

Borman shrugged. "We can't hold onto this ranch much longer, George. The Mexican government knows we're implicated . . . sooner or later Federal troops will move in on us."

"What do you want?"

"Your signature on a paper," Cass replied. "Giving me only what is mine anyway. A partnership in the Triangle T ranch."

Taine considered. It was true . . . the time had come to pull up stakes in Mexico, move back across the border. There no longer was need for this place . . . no need for further risk of running contraband. The Triangle T was big enough and he had enough money.

He nodded. "What about Maria?"

"I'll take some men to Durango," Cass said, "and get her out before the fighting starts."

George studied Borman, knowing he had to trust this man—he had no other choice.

"We've worked together a long time," he muttered. "About Maria—that's a promise, Cass?"

Borman said: "It's a promise."

George walked to his desk and sat down, taking out paper and pen . . . he wrote quickly, then dried the paper, handed it up to Borman.

Cass read it, nodded, then: "One thing, George. Date it two years back." His smile was cold. "I don't want it to appear like a last minute deal."

Taine shrugged. He dated it the way Cass wanted it and Borman added his signature to the agreement.

He said: "This satisfies me, George."

He went to the small table by the window, glanced out. Brazos Red was in the shadows, smoking. Cass nodded his head slightly, turned as George came up.

"Let's drink on it," he said. "To a new deal for both of us in Texas."

He handed George his glass, picked up his own. He raised it to the level of his eyes.

George said: "To a new deal—"

The shot came through the window glass, tearing into Taine's chest, just below his upraised arm. The big man staggered, dropped his glass . . . he turned and saw Brazos Red just outside the window, a gun in his hand and then his glazing eyes went to Borman and he knew

in that brief moment before death that Cass had won it all. . . .

The Mexican servants were clustered around Borman as he knelt by Taine's body. They looked on dispassionately; they were not involved.

Nor were the hired Mexican hands who worked the ranch. They had a loyalty to Maria, but she had gone with Avilla. And none of them cared to cross Cass Borman.

Cass pointed to the shattered glass. "The shot came from outside. There is a traitor among you . . . I will see that he is hanged!"

The servants listened stolidly, not believing, but doing nothing. They placed Taine's body on his bed and left.

Cass went to Taine's desk, folded the partnership agreement and tucked it into his coat pocket. There were several places where he could get the paper witnessed and notarized before he showed up at the Triangle T in Texas with a sad tale of a revolution that went wrong and the unfortunate death of his partner, George Taine.

Brazos Red and two other hard-eyed Texas gunslingers were waiting for him outside. They were mounted . . . Brazos held the reins of Borman's horse.

"We're going to Durango!" Cass said. And then, smiling: "Something I promised George Taine!"

No one made a move to stop them as they swung away from the ranch house, rode off into the night.

XIII

Durango sprawled on a windswept, dusty plain, baking under the afternoon sun. Goats ran untethered through the alleys and *calles* of the town, as did various species of chickens, some of them as wild as desert grouse.

The town lay astride the main road north out of Mexico City and it was a center of commerce for most of the high desert area. No other settlement of consequence lay within a hundred miles . . . whoever held it would control most of Chihuahua and Sonora.

The local *jefe*, Camillo, met Avilla and his party in the plaza . . . he came forward mopping his forehead with a red bandanna, a fleshy, middle-aged man in rumpled clothes. He knew who Avilla was, and why he was here, but he was powerless to do anything about it.

The mounted *Americanos* with Avilla made sure of this. He glanced at the wagons and smiled at Maria, but his heart wasn't in it.

"Quarters for these men," Avilla directed. "A place for my niece, Maria."

Camillo nodded vigorously. "Of course . . . of course . . ." He gestured to one of several men lounging in front of a cantina. "Fetch Paola . . ."

The man disappeared inside and Camillo turned back to Avilla.

89

"You are staying in Durango—?"

"Until General Franco arrives," Avilla said.

Camillo swallowed hard. "The *Generale* has already made arrangements by courier . . . his men are to be quartered—"

"We are here first!" Avilla cut him off. He was smiling, but his eyes were hard and Camillo nodded again.

"Of course. This way . . ." He pointed. "The *Cantina Delgado* for your men. My humble home, Vincente . . . if you will honor me . . . for you and Maria. . . ."

Avilla nodded, turned to Roger Briscole. "He is an American newspaperman," he said. "He will stay with us . . ."

The mounted column coming up out of the garrison just outside of Mexico City moved steadily, watched along the road by silent old men and children. The detachment had three French artillery pieces and the mounted troopers were among the best of the Mexican Army.

The man who led them was beefy, in his early forties, not much inclined to pomp and social activities. He was a career Army man who had studied military science in France and Spain and, later, in Prussia.

There was unrest in Mexico, General Franco knew, but it had not seriously involved any of his troopers; their loyalty could be depended on.

He had only contempt for the ragged revolutionaries he would face in Chihuahua.

He did not expect a long campaign.

Maria stood on the veranda of Camillo's house, looking across the walled garden to the low hills through which General Franco would come.

Avilla was with her.

He said quietly: "I wish you hadn't come, Maria."

She turned to him. "I have been with you since I left school—I couldn't stay behind now!"

He sighed. "That American, Cass Borman. Are you in love with him?"

She frowned. "I am in love with no one."

He nodded. "I am glad." He looked off. "He would not make you happy, Maria."

She shrugged.

"There is no one . . . no man . . . ?"

She looked at her uncle directly. "The revolution has been my only concern."

He shook his head. "It is not enough, Maria." His voice was gentle. "For some men, yes . . . but for a woman . . ." He shook his head again. "A woman does not fall in love with a revolution."

"There will be time," she answered diffidently, "after General Franco is beaten."

He looked off toward the hills again, pondering. "I don't know," he said slowly. "We have made mistakes . . . we are not liked everywhere." He glanced back to the house. "That American newspaperman in there . . . he called us bandits . . ."

She blazed: "What does he know? Has he seen the

91

suffering . . . the poverty of the people . . . the arrogance of those in power . . . ?"

He smiled and touched her cheek with the back of his hand. "Perhaps it should be you to lead us, Maria." His hand dropped. "Lately I've had a feeling . . . a bad feeling . . ."

"We have the guns!" she said intensely. "That is enough!"

He looked up at the sun, nodded. "Tomas and the others should be in position now. General Franco will march straight to Durango . . . he will not be expecting trouble here . . . all around us is an open plain. I know what he will be thinking—a ragged bunch of peasants, badly trained, armed with inferior weapons . . . he is thinking he will have to chase us into the hills . . ."

He stood for a long moment occupied with his thoughts, then he turned to her. "Stay in the house, Maria. I will go see how the Americans are doing."

Roger Briscole came out of the house and stopped beside Maria as Avilla left.

He was silent for a moment, then he said quietly: "I hope he wins, Maria."

She glanced quickly at him.

He smiled at the look in her eyes. "But I'll never get to write the story, will I?"

She said angrily: "Why not?"

"You don't know?" He was surprised.

"You've never believed in Uncle Vince's revolution, that's what I know. To you we're just bandits—"

He cut her off. "Not you, Maria." He looked off, the way Avilla had gone. "Not Vincente Avilla, either. Or those men last night, in that village . . ." He paused. "At first that's what I did think. The *Amigos*," he smiled faintly, "do not have a good reputation along the Texas border."

She said: "You'll write your story, Roger. By tomorrow morning, after General Franco is defeated—"

He shook his head. "Either way, win or lose, I won't be leaving here alive, Maria. Your father and Cass Borman will have seen to that."

"My father!"

He nodded. "I was a prisoner at your father's ranch," he said. "There was always a guard at my window. And Borman told me bluntly I'd be shot if I tried to leave."

She couldn't believe it. "Why?"

"Because I found out too much," he said. "I found out your father and Borman were using the revolution as an excuse to keep attention from their running of contraband across the border into the Triangle T."

He looked off toward the distant hills. "Neither Borman nor your father really care about what happens here today. They've used Avilla . . . now they're through with him . . ."

She backed away from him, not believing what he was saying—not wanting to believe.

"No!" she cried. "It's a lie—"

"Why should I lie?" he cut in bitterly. "What have I to gain?"

"How—how could you know?"

"It's my job to know—to find out the truth." He smiled, but it was at himself, as he said: "I have an unlimited expense account . . . and you'd be surprised at what money, in the right places, can bring out. Even at your father's *Paseo Grande* ranch—"

"It's not true," she said harshly. "If you were a prisoner, as you say, surely someone back in the United States, your newspaper—"

"Is not yet alarmed," he cut in. "Cass Borman has seen to that. He's been sending back stories, from a small border town called Ansara, in my name."

She stared at him, stricken. "No," she said, but her voice was a weak protest. "Borman, maybe. But my father wouldn't—"

Roger cut in gently: "I'm sorry I won't be able to prove any of this to you, Maria. But I've got a feeling that Borman has arranged it so that neither you nor I will be leaving Durango—"

He turned to go back into the house, but stopped abruptly, fear flaming across his face, as he saw the tall man in the doorway.

Cass Borman chuckled coldly. "Strange, isn't it, the things a man hears about himself behind his back?"

He made a motion and Brazos Red moved swiftly toward Roger . . . the correspondent turned and tried to run. Brazos drew his Colt and fired almost casually.

Roger Briscole was halfway across the yard, toward

the gate . . . the bullet sent him stumbling forward, on his face.

Borman looked at the white-faced girl. "You didn't really believe a word of what he said, did you, Maria?"

She backed away from him, a shocked numbness in her eyes.

"Cass," she whispered . . . "why?" She turned to look at Roger, lying still where he had fallen. "Oh, God, why?"

"You wouldn't want him getting back to the United States with the wrong kind of story, now would you, Maria?"

She stared at him, wondering what was behind that small smile, feeling revolted at the casualness with which Roger Briscole had been shot.

"You—didn't have to kill him," she said. She was moving back, getting ready to run.

Cass moved his head slightly to Brazos Red and the redheaded gunman moved in behind her, blocking her off.

Cass said quietly, "You're not afraid of me, are you, Maria?"

"I never was," she said bitterly, "until now." She looked past him, to the door. "Did father come with you? Or was Roger right about him, too—?"

"Your father is dead," Cass said bluntly.

She stared at him, a horror in her eyes.

"Oh, come on now, Maria," he said harshly. "He never meant much to you. It was your uncle Vince and his two-bit revolution you cared about."

"You—killed him?"

He shrugged. "Doesn't matter who killed him, Maria." He smiled coldly. "But I promised I'd take you out of Durango before General Franco got here."

"No," she said harshly. "I'm not leaving Durango—"

Brazos Red moved quickly at Cass' nod . . . he came up behind Maria and when she started to scream he clapped a hand over her mouth.

She fought wildly, with greater strength than Brazos had imagined—she almost got free of him before Borman, coming up, struck her across the face with the back of his hand.

She sagged then, staring at him with pained eyes, hating him.

Gabe Beaver, one of the two other men with Borman and Brazos came to the door behind Cass. He said, "The horses are ready, Mr. Borman."

Borman glanced at him, nodded. He turned back to Maria, his voice cold now, definite.

"I'm saving your life," he said. "Some day you'll thank me for it."

Brazos said: "What about the others, Mr. Borman? Gordon, Nogales, Cobb Eaton and—"

"They're being paid to fight," Borman said grimly. He looked off, toward the hills. "This time they'll earn their pay!"

XIV

THE AMERICANS had taken over the *Cantina Delgado*, Avilla noticed when he entered . . . they were scattered around the tables, most of them killing time with cards, a few going over their guns. They were a quiet group . . . professionals, they were being paid to fight. They would celebrate later—after the fighting was over.

The *cantina* girls had departed, taking refuge with friends in other parts of town. Many of the more frightened townspeople had fled into the hills. Only Paola, a rotund, usually jovial man remained behind the bar in the *cantina*, keeping an uneasy eye on these hard-faced mercenaries.

The boss of the *Amigos* put his quick, restless glance on the man he knew as Galahad, standing alone at the bar, a beer at his elbow. This man disturbed Avilla . . . he couldn't quite put his finger on what it was, but he knew the quick-tempered man did not belong with these others.

Gordon was seated at a table, playing poker with Nogales Smith, Cobb Eaton and Nat Hines. They had come into Mexico together and they usually kept together.

The ugly-faced *segundo* turned as Avilla came into the *cantina*. Like most Texans Gordon was inclined to

think little of the fighting prowess of Mexicans, but he had a lot of respect for this man.

He said: "How much longer, Vince?"

Avilla glanced around the room. "Latest word I receieved they were less than two hours' march away."

One of the men at another table, a tough blond kid named Jaster, said arrogantly: "About time."

Avilla nodded. "They should be showing up here just before sundown." He paused, studying these cold-eyed men, knowing how much he depended on them.

"I'll be joining my men just outside of town. Gordon will be in charge here . . ."

He looked over that silent, waiting group—no one raised any objections to this. But he noticed a cool cynicism in the eyes of many.

"I know," he said slowly, "that none of you is here because of a love for me, or Mexico. You are here because you are being paid well. So, I will appeal to what is important to you. If you fight well, in addition to the bonus Cass Borman has promised you, I will personally see that you are handsomely paid. If we lose—" he shrugged, his face grim, "well, General Franco will attend to that—"

Jaster said contemptuously: "Don't worry about us. We'll do the fighting. You just keep your men out of our line of fire—"

Avilla turned, studied the cocky young gunman for a moment, holding back the rise of his anger.

Gordon said, hard: "Shut up, Jaster!"

Jaster gave him a look; he was just wild enough to challenge Gordon if he was pushed.

Avilla cut in: "Franco won't be expecting trouble here—not at this time. His men will be tired from the long march—he's expecting to put them up in Durango." He paused. "Your job will be to stop them outside of town."

Gordon frowned. "What about those field guns he's got, Vince?"

"This is an open town," Avilla replied. "General Franco will think twice before using them on helpless people."

"And what will you be doing?" Jaster sneered.

Avilla looked at him. "We'll hit them from the rear—"

Jaster laughed contemptuously. "Figgers. That's about the safest place to be, ain't it? Behind the enemy—?"

Avilla moved swiftly, reaching Jaster before the gunman had time to get up. He backhanded him across the face, spilling him backward. He waited as Jaster, humiliated and raging mad, lunged to his feet and clawed for his gun.

Avilla drew and cocked his gun, beating Jaster by a mile . . . he came within a hair-trigger's breadth of killing him.

Gordon's quick voice stopped him: "Vince! He's just a damn fool kid!"

Jaster's hand moved away from his gun; he stared at Avilla, a thin fear in his eyes.

Slowly Avilla said: "Sit down!"

Jaster straightened his chair, sat down.

Gordon said harshly: "If he makes another damn fool move like that, Vince, *I'll* kill him!"

Avilla let out a tight, angry breath; he nodded. "You just hold them, Gordon. My men will do the rest of the fighting."

Gordon nodded: "We'll hold them!"

He waited until Avilla had left, then he put his gaze on every man in that room.

"We signed on to fight for Vince. And we're gonna hold this town, if it takes every last man of us!"

Gordon settled back in his chair and picked up his cards. "Come on," he growled to Nat Hines, who was dealing. "We got about an hour left. I want to win back the seventy bucks I lost."

At the bar Jeff was growing impatient. He couldn't make a move against Gordon in this room, and he had decided to take Roger Briscole with him when he left. This was part of the job his brother Ben had started—

He caught Nogales' eyes and frowned and Nogales nodded slightly. It was time to go.

Cobb Eaton chuckled as he laid down three aces. He looked across the table to Nogales.

Nogales said: "That beats me, Cobb," and tossed his hand into the discards.

He started to get up.

Gordon said coldly: "Where you going?"

Nogales shrugged. "Outside." He banged his knuckles gently against his chest. "Damn cigar smoke in here is getting to me."

"Sit down," Gordon said.

Cobb grinned. "Yeah—keep playing, Nogales." He checked a piece of paper on which he had been making notations. "Way I got it figgered you owe me one hundred and sixty three pesos—American."

"Take it out of my bonus," Nogales said casually. He looked at Gordon. "I've had enough, Silent. I'm going out for a few minutes . . ."

A small suspicion glinted in Gordon's eyes. He nodded, looked across the room to Jeff.

"Join us, Galahad?"

Jeff said: "I don't play poker."

Gordon made a command motion with his thumb. "Join us anyway!"

Jeff stiffened. The man was pushing him and he saw Nogales lick his lips and shake his head slightly.

Nogales intervened. "Aw, come on, Galahad—take my place for a while. Maybe you'll have better luck."

Jeff shrugged. He watched Nogales go out the back door, then crossed to Gordon's table and sat down in Nogales' chair.

Gordon said idly: "You an' that runt Nogales have been pretty thick, lately. . . ."

Jeff eyed him. Nat Hines was dealing again. Jeff let his cards lay in front of him.

Gordon picked up his hand. He studied them, his voice casual. "You're pretty good with a hand gun, Galahad. We'll find out how good you are with a rifle, when that Mex Army shows up."

Jeff shrugged. "I'll earn my pay," he said. He pushed

his cards away. "I said I didn't play." He started to get up.

Gordon's right hand came up with his Colt . . . he rested his hand on the table, the muzzle pointed at Jeff.

"Cigar smoke getting to you, too?"

Jeff's lips tightened.

Gordon kept his bright blue gaze on Jeff. Aside he said to Cobb Eaton: "Keep an eye on him. I'm gonna check on Nogales."

Cobb drew his gun . . . the others in the room watched with varying degrees of indifference. This was an intramural quarrel, they felt, and they had no stake in it.

Jeff watched Gordon get up and walk quickly across the room to exit through the rear door.

Cobb Eaton said dryly: "Pick up your cards, Galahad. If you don't know how to play, we'll teach you!"

His voice was casual, but the gun in his hand was steady, and it was pointed at Jeff's chest.

XV

NOGALES SMITH worked quickly, saddling his horse and Jeff's big roan which were stabled with the others in the long adobe structure behind Delgado's *cantina*. At the last moment he had gone into the stable's corral to

pick out two pack mules . . . he didn't mind stealing from the Mexicans, but he had a streak of loyalty where it concerned the men he had been working with.

Now he was fastening the first of two big water canteens to one of the pack animals. It would take all the water they could carry, he was thinking, to get them across the Sonoran deserts.

He paused as he heard a man's step behind him and, thinking it was Galahad, he said: "Glad you could get away—"

He was turning his head as he said this; he stopped, his voice cutting off in a sharp gasp as he saw Gordon lounging against the door framing.

There was a gun in Gordon's hand, and it was held, casually but very directly, at Nogales.

Gordon said, humorlessly: "Cigar smoke was too much for you, eh?" He sniffed the ammonia-pungent air of the stable. "Doesn't smell a whole lot better in here, Nogales."

The small outlaw shrugged; he said nervously: "Hell, I just came in to check the horses—"

Gordon cut him off, his voice cold: "*Two* horses—yours and Galahad's!" He glanced at the pack mules. "And I see you picked out a couple of pack animals, too." His chuckle sent a chill down Nogales' back—he knew this man too well.

"Who were you expecting?"

Nogales said: "Nobody—" and checked himself as Gordon started to walk toward him.

He said in a low, desperate voice: "Cripes, Gordon —don't you believe me?"

Gordon shook his head. He cocked the hammer of his .45 Colt back as he walked and Nogales backed away from him . . . the small man kept backing up until he felt the hard press of stall boards stop him.

Gordon said: "I don't believe you one bit, Nogales. I figger you're planning to run out on me."

He stopped by one of the pack mules, hefted the canteen hanging from the saddle. "Water, too." His cold and deadly gaze fastened on the small man. "Who was going with you, Nogales?"

Nogales eyed the cocked gun in Gordon's hand. He knew lying would get him nowhere with this man.

"Galahad," he said.

"Two pack animals and water," Gordon reflected grimly. "Which way were you headed?"

Nogales licked his dry lips. "I won't lie to you, Gordon. We planned to leave, right after the fighting." This was a small lie and he figured he could get away with it. "Galahad said he'd split with me—"

"Split what?"

"Money he stole—stage holdup out of El Paso, I think. He's got it hid out there, somewhere just north of where we picked him up in Escondido Valley."

"Just you and Galahad, eh?" Gordon's voice was low, chiding—he was the kind of man who pulled wings off butterflies.

Nogales said, without thinking: "I was planning to cut you in on it, Gordon—"

He cringed as he saw Gordon's thumb move back on the hammer. "All right," he said desperately, "I was going it alone with Galahad. I didn't figger you'd miss me—"

Gordon reached out and slapped him across the face with the gun. The metal split Nogales' cheek; he fell against the stall boards and went to his knees.

"Goes to show," Gordon said contemptuously, "you ride with a man for better than seven years an' you never really get to know him."

Nogales pushed himself up to his feet. "You, Cobb, Nat an' me," he said thickly. "We've been close. But I'm older than all of you—not many more days living off my gun for me—"

He took out his handkerchief and held it to the blood coming from the cut on his cheek.

"Ten thousand dollars, Galahad said—my share. Enough for an old man like me. . . ."

Gordon said: "Well, maybe you're right, Nogales." He was thinking he had found a way to kill Galahad, as he had been instructed, without arousing the other men . . . they were adventurers, gunmen who fought for anyone who would hire them—but they had their own code of ethics. They wouldn't stand for anyone shooting another man in the back.

He lowered his gun. "I don't like the setup here, either." He made a motion toward the unseen hills. "And I've got a feeling Vince isn't going to make it." He scowled. "And you know what'll happen to us, if that Mex general wins. A firing squad!"

Nogales eyed him, relieved but not quite sure which way Gordon was leaning.

Gordon said: "Get Galahad out here. I'm riding with you."

Nogales licked his lips. "I don't think Galahad will—"

"He'll cut me in, too," Gordon cut him off, his voice harsh, "or neither one of you will leave here alive!"

Nogales hesitated, a sinking feeling in his stomach. That was one of the curses of riding with a man a long time—you got to know when he was lying. And Gordon was lying now. Gordon was not the kind of man who'd settle for a third of thirty thousand dollars when he could get it all. Nor was he the sort to forget an insult or a humiliation. Gordon had a mean streak a mile long—Nogales knew he hated Galahad for what Galahad had done to him back at the Paseo Grande. And he knew, too, that Gordon would not forget what Nogales had been about to do—

Gordon lifted his gun again. "Get him out here, Nogales!"

Nogales nodded, knowing he had no choice.

"Stand in the doorway and call him," Gordon directed. "I'll be right here, looking down your back!"

Jeff picked up his cards and glanced at them . . . he had been playing without much interest, but strangely enough, his luck had been running wild. He had already won the last three hands and he saw now that he was holding a full house—kings and tens.

Cobb Eaton had placed his gun on the table in front

of him . . . he was studying his cards, holding them close to his vest. Cobb took his poker seriously.

Nat pulled out his pocket watch. "Getting close to that time," he said. He looked at Cobb. "Wonder what's keeping Gordon—?"

He was facing the back door and he saw Nogales open it and stand there, looking in.

Nat said: "Well, Nogales is back, anyway—"

Jeff turned and glanced at the small outlaw. Nogales was still holding his handkerchief to his cheek.

Nogales said: "Galahad, come out here. Something I want to show you—"

Cobb put a hand on his gun. He said to Jeff: "You stay right here." He looked at Nogales. "Where's Gordon?"

"In the stable. He wants to see Galahad. Something about his horse. . . ."

Cobb frowned. "Don't sound like Gordon—"

Nat Hines cut in: "Hell, what do you care, Cobb? If Nogales says he wants Galahad—"

Cobb shifted his glance from Jeff to Nogales for a moment and Jeff's hand snaked across the table, clamping on his gun hand, twisting the muzzle away from him. He lunged erect in the same move, his own Colt coming up, muzzling Cobb.

"If you don't mind," he said grimly.

He twisted the gun from Cobb's hand, slid it to Hines. "I don't want to kill anybody just to quit a poker game," he said. He nodded toward Nogales. "I'll just go see what he wants."

He eased his gun back into his holster and walked to the back door.

Nogales moved back into the alley as Jeff came up—Jeff kicked the back door shut.

He said coldly: "Where's Gordon?" And because he was keyed up, expecting a doublecross, he moved the instant he saw Gordon ease into sight in the doorway of the stable fifty yards up the alley.

Gordon's shot burned across his upper arm . . . he was moving when Gordon fired and he tripped and fell against the *cantina* wall and went down to his knees.

Nogales spun around, knowing he was next . . . he got his gun out and he fired once, hastily, before Gordon's bullets cut him down.

The ugly-faced man came down the alley, his gun smoking . . . he thought he had Jeff and he reacted too late as Jeff rolled aside and fired.

The slugs knocked Gordon back against the adobe wall . . . he was dead as he started to slide down.

Jeff knelt by Nogales' side. The man was dying.

He said: "Sorry, Nogales. Looks like we won't make it to Guaymas . . ."

Nogales sighed. "Guess we won't . . ." His eyes closed. "Aw, hell," he whispered. "Ten thousand dollars . . ."

The *cantina's* back door opened cautiously and Cobb Eaton looked out, a gun in his hand. Jeff's quick shot chipped adobe a foot from his head and he ducked back inside, slamming the door shut.

Jeff turned, ran into the stable. The roan was sad-

dled and ready to go. He vaulted aboard, rode him out, went galloping down the alley. . . .

The hard-faced mercenaries were grouped around Nogales in the alley. Nat Hines knelt beside the older man . . . he glanced at Cobb who was standing by Gordon's body.

"Nogales is still alive," he said.

Cobb walked back to him, looked down at Nogales. The dying man opened his eyes.

Cobb said: "What happened?"

Nogales thought a moment. He was past pain now . . . he felt himself beginning to slip away.

He said, his voice barely above a whisper: "Gordon —went crazy, I guess. Made me call Galahad out—then tried to kill him. Shot me, too . . ."

Cobb said grimly: "Galahad got away?"

Nogales' head rolled. "He's hurt—don't know how bad." His eyes steadied on Cobb's face. "Let him go, Cobb. He . . . he's not one of us, anyway . . ."

Cobb looked back to Gordon's body. Nat Hines said: "Looks like Gordon asked for it, Cobb."

Cobb nodded slowly. He turned and eyed the others.

"We got a choice to make. We can cut out—or stay."

Jaster let his hand slide down to his gun. "I told Vince Avilla we'd hold this town. I don't want no damn Mex saying I cut out an' ran from a bunch of greasers, even if they are part of the Mex army!"

This seemed, somehow, the sentiment of all of them. Cobb shrugged.

"Well, General Franco's boys should be showing up any time now. Let's go earn our bonus!"

XVI

ROGER BRISCOLE dragged himself slowly up the steps of Don Camillo's house and paused in the doorway, fighting off a wave of pain and nausea. The bullet had struck him high up in the back and glanced off his shoulder blade . . . he had lain still, playing dead, knowing that any movement would have brought another bullet.

Maria's cut-off scream still lingered in his head—he peered now into the darker reaches of the house, seeing no one.

Don Camillo and his wife had been at home, he knew . . . he called out, his voice cracking with the effort. No one answered him.

I'm going to die, he thought and a twinge of self-pity went through him. Here, in a small Mexican village on a windswept, dusty plain moments before a small and quite insignificant battle for power was to take place.

He had a story to write, but it was not this one— the story he wanted to write was of an American expatriate named Cass Borman and the men he had used—George Taine and Vincente Avilla.

And the men he had left to die here in Durango.

The wave of nausea ebbed and he moved into the house, supporting himself every few steps by leaning against the wall. And then, coming into the big room off the entrance hall he saw why Don Camillo had not answered him.

He closed his eyes, recoiling from the sight—the utter savagery of the scene repelling him. They were dead, both of them—their throats cut.

Cass Borman, he thought, was ruthlessly thorough. Win or lose, Vincente Avilla and his American mercenaries would be blamed for these deaths.

He heard the rider come into the yard and he pushed himself away from the wall, a wild thought ricocheting through his head. *Was it one of Borman's men, come back to make sure he was dead . . . ?*

He tried to run, to find a place to hide . . . he stumbled and fell and lay there, for the moment too weak too rise. . . .

Jeff Corrin came into the house and paused as he saw Roger Briscole lying on the floor of the entrance hall. He had followed a small trail of blood from the garden . . . he drew his gun now as he went to the newspaperman's side, knelt beside him.

Roger looked at him, blinking. Then, relieved: "Galahad . . . thank God . . ."

Jeff cut in grimly: "Where's Maria?"

"Borman," Roger said weakly. He tried to get up, managing to get to one knee. "He came—with some

111

men. Brazos Red . . . shot me. They took Maria away."

"When?"

"About ten . . . fifteen minutes . . ." Roger waved toward the living room. "They killed Camillo . . . his wife . . ."

Jeff considered. He had come for Roger and Maria; he figured he didn't have much time to decide what to do now. He didn't know if Cobb Eaton and the others wouldn't be coming after him—at any rate General Franco would be showing up about now.

It wasn't his fight, he thought . . . it was not what he had come into Mexico for.

He looked at Roger. "How bad are you hurt?"

Roger started to get up, his face twisted with pain. "Right shoulder," he said. "Can't move my arm much . . ."

Jeff ripped his coat off. He saw where Brazos' bullet had gone in and come out . . .

"You're lucky," he said grimly.

He went through the house, found some sheets which he tore into bandages, came back with a bottle of brandy. "Grit your teeth," he said. He poured some of the brandy into the raw bullet holes and Roger gasped, fell back. Jeff put his arm under his head and forced some of the brandy down Roger's throat.

The newspaperman gagged, opened his eyes.

Jeff fastened a rough bandage over the wound, then helped Roger to his feet. "I've got a mule outside," he said. "Think you can ride?"

Roger nodded.

With Jeff's help they went out into the garden. The

pack mule was still tied to Jeff's saddle on a lead rope. Jeff helped the wounded man aboard.

"Hang on as long as you can," he instructed. "When it gets too tough, yell out."

Roger said: "Where we going?"

"North," Jeff answered shortly. "I'm taking you back across the border. . . ."

Tomas squatted by his horse, chewing on a desert twig. A hundred men waited with him, armed with shiny new rifles . . . they fingered loaded bandoliers as they waited, their eyes bright, expectant. There was no talking—only the silence of men waiting to go into battle.

Avilla came back to him, field glasses in his hands . . . he stuffed them into his saddle bags.

"The Americans . . . ?" Tomas asked.

"They are ready," Avilla answered.

Tomas grunted. "It will be quick, then." He tossed the twig away. "What shall we do with General Franco?"

Avilla looked off. "What he would do to us—if we lose."

Tomas grinned as he made a swift motion of cutting his throat—

A man came down the line, moving quickly. "They are on time," he said. "If you look, you can see their dust . . . there . . . just below the hill . . ."

Avilla nodded, looked at Tomas. "Just a few minutes more," he said.

113

Tomas' eyes glittered. "It's the waiting that is hard, Vincente. . . ."

The Americans waited behind the low wall facing the road to Mexico City. Only ten now, rifles ready, eyes slitted—watching the road into the distant hills.

Cobb Eaton, who had taken command of the small group, said: "Hope Vince doesn't take too long . . ."

Jaster spat out the shredded butt of his cigarette. "A hundred Mex troopers, Cobb? Hell, we can hold them off all night, if we have to!"

The Mexican cavalry column moved down the long slant of ground toward Durango. The three French artillery guns rattled along behind. The column moved with the precision of trained soldiers.

As Avilla had predicted, General Franco was not expecting trouble. But he was a military man, and a good one—and he was never careless.

He moved up along the column, the stub of a short, black cigar in a corner of his mouth, and halted it when he was still a quarter of a mile from town. He studied the clustered adobes of Durango through his field glasses. The town was too quiet . . . it looked deserted.

He turned and called a lieutenant to his side. "Take a half dozen men," he ordered. "Scout the town. Find out why the *jefe*, Camillo, isn't coming out to meet us."

The lieutenant saluted. He picked out six men . . . they rode toward Durango.

Cobb Eaton watched them come. He had not counted on this. He wondered if it might not be better to let this advance patrol enter the town. Then—

But Avilla had given strict orders. *Hold Durango!*

He said calmly: "Well, this is it. We'll wait until they're within range. Don't miss!"

The patrol rode at a jog toward Durango. When they were within a hundred yards the Americans fired. All seven men were killed in that first volley. . . .

Watching, General Franco clamped his teeth down hard on his cigar.

"All right," he said harshly, "no quarter . . ."

He relayed orders to his guns. Quickly and efficiently they wheeled the artillery pieces around, muzzles pointing toward Durango.

The first volley was high, exploding into the buildings behind the Americans.

As the gunners reloaded, the troopers flanked out, prepared to charge. . . .

Avilla and Tomas were already mounted . . . they gave a command signal and the hundred eager men swept out of the gully and charged the Mexican column.

It should have worked. General Franco was caught by surprise and for a moment his line of command was thrown into confusion.

Then the confusion swept back into the ranks of the

charging revolutionaries as the shiny new rifles they had waited so long for did not fire.

For every *Amigo* whose Winchester fired there were four which did not.

The veteran troopers from Mexico City rallied and charged the suddenly confused and helpless revolutionaries—who broke and tried now only to escape. Methodically and efficiently the troopers shot them down . . . chasing them back into the gully.

Tomas was killed at the first volley, clutching a rifle that didn't work. He died turning to look at Avilla, a shocked and bitter question in his eyes—a question Avilla could not answer, had no time to answer . . .

He fired his weapon and kept firing, but he knew his cause was lost, and he cursed Cass Borman wildly, knowing in these final tragic moments how he had been betrayed.

The rifle bullet hit him in the stomach and went through him . . . he felt the burn of it like a red hot poker in his insides and he fell forward, losing his rifle, clutching at his horse's mane. The animal was running wildly now, heading for the hills.

All around him men were falling, yelling . . . horses ran by without riders. Avilla hung on, only half conscious, thinking of Borman . . . there was only one terrible thought left in his mind. He wanted to stay alive . . . he wanted to live just long enough to get his hands around Cass Borman's neck. . . .

General Franco sat his horse and watched the slaughter without expression, the cigar clamped firmly in a

corner of his mouth. The artillery was lobbing shells toward Durango . . . he ordered them to cease firing.

He shook his head. A rabble, he thought—nothing but a rabble. He looked toward the town which was now strangely quiet.

His troopers re-formed . . . their losses against Avilla had been extremely light.

At Franco's signal they rode into Durango. The ten men trapped in the town never had a chance. . . .

XVII

FROM HIGH up in the desert hills Jeff and Roger viewed the battle for Durango . . . it seemed an unreal, distant stage play of toy soldiers and barely heard crackling of rifles. The heavier explosions of the artillery were like hollow poppings punching through the dying day.

They witnessed the rout of Avilla and his men, although neither Jeff nor Roger could understand why it had failed so dismally. And when the Mexican troopers under General Franco re-formed and went charging into Durango, Jeff and Roger turned and rode away.

They camped that night somewhere north of Durango, on a slope just above a deep and rock-strewn arroyo. There were clouds gathering in the south, moving toward them, and Jeff knew the desert country well

enough to know what a flash flood roaring down that arroyo could do. Rain came suddenly here, and in torrents, and, sometimes, even when the sun was shining. The land was gullied and torn and constantly being reshaped . . . it was the same land that ran up into western Texas and Arizona and New Mexico . . . dry and forbidding and sparsely populated.

They rested around a small fire of *piñon* nuts and branches. Neither felt very hungry, but in any case they had nothing to eat. Jeff was thankful for the canteen Nogales had fastened to the mule's saddle.

Roger's back and right shoulder had stiffened. He lay with his head pillowed on a saddle, a folded blanket under his back to ease the discomfort . . . he watched Jeff hunkered down by the fire, the flames outlining the ex-Ranger's hard face. The blood had dried around the bullet cut on Jeff's arm—if it bothered him he did not show it.

"I've seen you before," Roger said. "You're not Galahad. Who are you?"

Jeff shrugged. "Jeff Corrin."

"Corrin?" Roger's brow knitted in thought. "I met a Texas Ranger named Corrin—"

"My brother Ben," Jeff said shortly. He tossed a couple of *piñon* nuts on the fire. "He was waiting for me in Ansara. I was to help him find out what happened to you. He was killed before I got there."

"Borman?"

"Borman was there," Jeff replied, "sending a wire

story to your paper, in your name. But it was Gordon who killed Ben. That's what Nogales said."

Roger nodded. "Of course." He looked at Jeff, interested. "Is that why you came into Mexico?"

Jeff thought a moment before replying. "My brother wanted me back in the Rangers. I . . ." He paused, thinking back. "I was just drifting . . ."

Roger said: "I remember now. You were a Ranger once— I think I remember reading about a trial . . ." He waited for Jeff to say something, but Jeff was looking into the fire. The memories Roger had recalled were not pleasant.

"What happened to Gordon?"

"I killed him," Jeff said. He did not elaborate, but added: "I guess the others are dead, too . . ."

"So is George Taine," Roger said. He saw by the way Jeff turned his head and looked at him that Jeff had not known.

"I heard Borman tell Maria. He killed Taine—or had him killed . . ." Roger paused and shifted his weight slightly, trying to ease his sore back.

"I'm sorry to hear about Taine," Jeff said. "He knew who I was, the moment he drove into the *Paseo Grande* yard. One word from him—" He took a long breath, staring into the campfire. "I think he knew then that Borman would kill him. He was practically a prisoner on his own ranch . . . he told me as much . . . and there was nothing I could do to help . . ."

Roger's voice was bitter: "Looks like Cass Borman won it all."

"Looks like it." Jeff stood up and gazed off into the darkness. "He's probably headed back for the *Paseo Grande* ..."

He turned back to Roger. "You wouldn't know how to get back there, would you?" The newspaperman grinned at the thought. Jeff saw the look on his face and smiled. "I don't, either. But maybe in the morning I can pick up their tracks. Borman can't be too far ahead of us ..."

Roger looked up at the stars, thinking. "The *Paseo Grande* won't be worth much to Borman, now that Taine is dead and Avilla and his *Amigos* wiped out. But the Triangle T would—"

He looked at Jeff, frowning. "I wonder why he came all the way to Durango for Maria?"

Jeff thought of the girl then, and said simply: "Some men want most what they can't get. ..."

Vincente Avilla rested through the hours of the night, curled up like a desert animal, one hand pressed to the hole in his stomach which now oozed only a little blood. The other was wrapped around the reins of his horse. He couldn't risk letting the animal get away from him—he knew he was dying ... knew it was only a matter of time.

He prayed, looking up at the stars ... he prayed for a chance to get to Borman before he slipped away into that distant eternity. At times he was delirious and thought he was riding again at the head of the *Amigos* ... he called out sharply: "Tomas ... ho,

Tomas!" and his horse, startled, moved away, dragging him several yards before Avilla came to and stopped him.

He slept fitfully after that, but the fever seemed to pass from his brain . . . when dawn stained the eastern horizon he dragged himself up into the saddle. He was chilled . . . he shivered as much from weakness, however, as from the desert cold.

He gazed up at the stars beginning to dim in the sky, getting his bearings by them—he knew which way to go to get to the *Paseo Grande*. That's where he was headed. He thought Cass Borman was still there.

Maria?

She came to his mind then and he almost turned back to Durango. She had always been with him for the revolution—and she had come with him to Durango. But he knew that nothing he could possibly do now could help her . . . he could only pray that General Franco would be lenient with her.

He took a small swallow of water from his canteen. His wound was still oozing blood . . . he knew he had only a limited time left. He slid his hand down the cold butt plate of his holstered gun and prayed for enough time to get to Borman.

The horse under him snorted as he turned north toward the distant *Paseo Grande*. . . .

Jeff Corrin and Roger were moving in an almost identical path, although Jeff was not so sure that he was headed in the right direction. This was new country

to him and although he tried to recognize landmarks, he knew that a mesa or a peak or even a jumble of rocks looked one way when approached from one direction and another when viewed from the opposite side.

He had not paid much attention to the trail from *Paseo Grande* to the abandoned village of Santa Lucia and finally to Durango because at that time he had not considered coming back this way.

But now he was being forced into reconsidering his position. He had avenged Ben's murder, but he had not finished Ben's job . . . it wouldn't be finished until he brought Cass Borman back across the border into Texas to stand trial in an American court.

For Borman had killed his brother Ben as surely as Gordon, who had pulled the trigger.

It was Roger who worried about Maria.

"Maybe that's why Borman came to Durango for her," he said, during a morning break. "Maybe, at first, he wanted her that badly. But—" He paused to reflect, pulling together what he knew of the man who had held him prisoner. "The way things stand now, with George Taine dead, he'll take over the Triangle T. That's where the money is, and the power. The *Paseo Grande* can't be held . . . the Mexican authorities know pretty well by now where Vince Avilla's support came from.

"He can get by with almost any story, once he gets into Texas . . . everyone knows of the trouble in northern Mexico . . . he could just say he was lucky to get back across the border alive . . .

"But if he takes Maria with him he'll have to share the Triangle T with her. And he'll never be sure she won't go to the district attorney with the real story of what happened . . . he'll never be sure of her—"

Jeff cut in: "You think he'll kill her?"

Roger shrugged. "He may be thinking that way now." He looked grim. "Borman's gotten everything he wanted, even Maria, so far—but he may be thinking he doesn't want her that much now . . ."

Jeff looked off into the long glaring reaches of desert ahead. Jagged hills ran like a sawtooth barrier across it.

Borman and his men could be somewhere just ahead . . . *but where?*

"I could get you back across the border," he told Roger. "But if we go after Borman—?"

He left it up to the newspaperman.

Roger tried to move his shoulder . . . it was stiff and it pained him. He smiled uncertainly. "I don't want to be a hero," he said slowly . . . "I'd much rather head straight for Texas. But—" he looked off, his newspaperman's mind working—"if we get Cass Borman, I'll have the story of a lifetime. . . ."

XVIII

BORMAN WAS camped in an old Mexican peasant's hut—a goat herder's place, abandoned when revolutionary unrest swept across this part of Mexico. A few of the goats still came back, for the small spring back of the stone and adobe hut was the only water for miles around.

The horse Maria had been riding had gone lame . . . somehow it had thrown a hind shoe during the early morning hours and the land they were crossing was hard on unshod hoofs. And, too, the canteen which had hung from Maria's saddle had disappeared . . . thinking about it now, Borman suspected that she had been the cause of both annoyances.

Not that Borman was in a hurry. He wasn't figuring on pursuit.

Brazos Red was dozing in the shade of the hut, his hat pulled down over his eyes, his back against the wall. He slept with his gloved hand resting on his gun butt . . . and he slept lightly, stirring at once as Borman took a step toward him.

The other two men were by a small campfire. Gabe Beaver, some fifty years old and whang leather tough was boiling water for coffee. He claimed to have been a mountain man with Fremont—Borman knew him as a liar and a cold-blooded killer. Gabe carried a hunt-

ing knife in a sheath at his belt—it had been he who had killed Camillo and his wife, with as little compunction as though he had been slitting the throat of a chicken.

Bill Gunning, the other man with Gabe, picking at his teeth, was younger by more than twenty years. He was a dull-witted man, so-so with a gun, but dependable.

Both men had been among the first Borman had hired on at the *Paseo Grande.*

He watched them for a long moment, like a man contemplating pawns on a chess board. And, like pawns, he figured they were expendable.

Nor, he reflected cold-bloodedly, did he need Maria. He had always been a man more occupied with other things than women . . . he took them, when it occurred to him, casually, his mind often on other things.

Maria had gotten to him because she was the most feminine woman he had seen in a long, long time—but mostly because she had always held him off. He had wanted her because he couldn't have her. Looking at her now, resting in the shade of a small *ramada,* he realized how dangerous it would be to take her with him into Texas.

He thought about this for a moment and then went inside the hut and picked up his rifle. It had been a long time since he had done his own killing.

He came to the doorway and looked toward Gabe . . . neither he nor Gunning noticed Borman. Brazos

Red was still dozing . . . Maria was staring off toward the near hills.

Borman raised his rifle and killed Gabe with his first shot. The man fell across the fire, spilling the coffee pot . . . fire licked up and around his body.

Gunning turned, a stunned look on his dull face. Borman's next shot spun him around. He fell, clawed the earth and the next shot snuffed out his life.

Borman lowered his rifle and looked into the muzzle of Brazos' gun.

"Put that away, Red," he said calmly.

Brazos came to his feet, the gun still leveled at Borman. He said: "You gone crazy?"

Borman glanced at Maria, who had come to her feet —she was staring at them, a hundred feet away.

Borman said almost casully: "No—just smart." He started to raise his rifle at Maria and Brazos snapped:
"Hold it, Cass!"

Borman said: "We don't need Gabe and Bill any more—we don't need her, either. With her out of the way I own all of the Triangle T—"

"And me?" Brazos cut in grimly. "Where do I fit in?"

"I need a man to help me run it," Borman said. He smiled placatingly. "Just you and me, making it across the border. Mexican bandits got the rest . . . including the girl . . . who'll question us, Red?"

He turned around again, his rifle leveling—but Maria was already on the run, heading toward the hills. Cass fired hurriedly, annoyed at his carelessness at having taken the time to talk to Brazos. He missed with the

first shot, but the second staggered Maria . . . she kept running, however, and disappeared into one of the innumerable erosion gullies that spider-webbed the dry land.

Borman was not too concerned. He reloaded without hurry. The smell of burning flesh wafted to him and he said: "Get Gabe out of there," to Brazos.

Brazos considered for a moment before obeying. The offer Borman had extended appealed to him, but he knew he would always have to be wary of this man.

He went over and pulled Gabe's body out of the fire and beat out the flames.

Borman said: "Saddle the horses. She's hurt—she can't get too far . . ."

He waited, watching Brazos, the rifle resting in the crook of his arm. *Getting rusty*, he thought . . . *once he could have killed her with his first shot. . . .*

Drooped over his horse's neck, Avilla heard the first rifle shots . . . he forced himself erect, fighting the grayness that was inexorably creeping into his brain.

He had been drifting this way—how long he wasn't sure. But the shots—?

He was at the base of a rocky slope, looking off across a baked plain . . . he could see someone running toward him—and someone else, in front of a stone hut standing alone on a desolate plain, firing again. The running figure disappeared, but he recognized the man who had been firing . . . savagely he dug his spurs

into his horse's flanks, sent him lunging toward the goat herder's shack.

A half mile east of Avilla, Jeff and Roger were riding down a wide wash. Jeff had earlier come across the tracks of five horses—they were recent and he felt they had to be Borman's party.

The rifle shots alerted him. He stood up in his stirrups and could just see over the bank of the wash . . . the goat herder's shack was less than a quarter of a mile away.

He recognized Maria, running . . . she disappeared, and then he saw Borman and Brazos Red mount and ride after her.

He drew his rifle and sent his horse lunging up the bank, not waiting for Roger Briscole. . . .

Avilla reached Maria first. She had staggered up out of the gully as he rode up . . . he saw her through a red haze and he did not even have time to be surprised. Up ahead, Cass Borman, riding in front of Brazos Red, pulled to a sudden stop, stark amazement on his face.

Avilla drew and fired. His shot killed Borman's horse. Borman went down with the animal and Avilla kept firing as he rode toward the man momentarily pinned under his mount . . . he emptied his gun at Borman—missing him in his haste, his desperation.

Borman pulled free and started to run . . . Avilla swept up beside him and lunged out of his saddle, his hands going for Borman's throat. They went down to-

gether and he was still on top of Borman when Brazos Red killed him.

Maria screamed.

Brazos swung around to her, his gun leveling . . . he jerked and fired quickly as he saw Jeff Corrin, seemingly coming out of nowhere, riding toward him. He fired again—Jeff's horse stumbled and Jeff rolled out of his saddle, Red's bullets kicking up sand around him. Jeff steadied himself briefly and fired at Brazos.

The gunman doubled . . . he dropped his Colt and then tried to pick it up . . . he died a few moments later, lying doubled over his gun, on the hot, baked earth.

Borman rolled free of Avilla's body only to find himself looking into Jeff's leveled gun. Behind Jeff he could see another rider coming toward them . . . a few moments later he recognized Roger Briscole.

He had it all, he thought numbly—*and had lost it all.*

Maria was kneeling over Avilla's body, crying . . . she looked up at Jeff.

"Galahad . . ." she said brokenly, "how . . . ?"

"The name's Corrin," he said quietly, "Jeff Corrin." He looked at Borman. "It's a long story, Maria . . . I'll tell it to you later . . . on the way back to Texas . . ."

They buried Vincente Avilla where he died, and where he would have wanted to be buried, on the parched and desolate plains of Mexico. They marked it with a wooden cross Jeff made from wood from the

goat herder's hut. Brazos Red, Gabe and Gunning were buried in a wash behind the shack.

Borman rode with his hands tied behind his back—ahead of Jeff and Roger. Maria rode between them . . . quiet, grieving. Her wound was slight; it was a deeper hurt that numbed her. In time the pain would ease . . . the pain of a revolution betrayed . . . dreams killed. But she would never forget.

The four of them moved out across that desolate land . . . they rode north, toward Texas.

Double the action, double the reading, with

ACE DOUBLE WESTERNS

71372 **THE HOSTILE PEAKS** by Louis Trimble
with **RENEGADE ROUNDUP** by Tom West

76900 **THE SKULL RIDERS** by Dean Owen
with **THE MAN WHO SHOT "THE KID"**
by Merle Constiner

09135 **CANYON WAR** by Sam Bowie
with **THE HOODED GUN** by Clay Ringold

86465 **ZERO HOUR AT BLACK BUTTE** by Don P. Jenison
with **SHERIFF OF SENTINEL** by Clement Hardin

30850 **THE GUNS OF SONORA** by Ben Smith
with **BLACK BUZZARDS OF BUENO** by Tom West

24925 **THE FOURTH GUNMAN** by Merle Constiner
with **SLICK ON THE DRAW** by Tom West

52035 **MARSHAL FROM WHISKEY SMITH** by Eric Allen
with **IMPOSTORS IN MESQUITE** by Gene Tuttle

14195 **DEATH WAITS AT DAKINS STATION**
by Merle Constiner
with **RANSOME'S DEBT** by Kyle Hollingshead

Two novels for the price of one

60¢ each double-book

(Include 10¢ handling fee per copy)

Order from Ace Books (Dept. MM), 1120 Ave. of the
Americas, New York, N.Y. 10036.

ACE high winners for Western reading!

Here's a list of leaders:

30750 — 60¢   **GUNDOWN** by Brian Wynne

71720 — 50¢   **RETURN TO BROKEN CROSSING**
by Lee Hoffman

52240 — 50¢   **THE MAVERICK STAR**
by L. P. Holmes

70000 — 60¢   **A QUINTET OF SIXES**
Donald A. Wollheim, Editor

32880 — 60¢   **A HERO FOR HENRY**
by Herbert R. Purdum

73435 — 60¢   **ROGUE'S LEGACY**
by L. L. Foreman

30400 — 60¢   **GRINGO**
by Nelson Nye

71150 — 60¢   **THE RED SABBATH**
by Lewis B. Patten

62730 — 60¢   **ONCE AN OUTLAW**
by Matt Kincaid

Order from Ace Books (Dept. MM), 1120 Avenue of the
Americas, New York, N.Y. 10036. Send price of book
indicated, plus 10¢ for handling.

Order by Book Number

The ACE brand means better Westerns by better writers.
Don't miss these: